# An Unrehearsed Desire

# AN
# UNREHEARSED
# DESIRE

## LAUREN B. DAVIS

*Exile Editions*

*Publishers of singular*
*Fiction, Poetry, Drama, Non-fiction and Graphic Books*
2008

Library and Archives Canada Cataloguing in Publication

Davis, Lauren B., 1955-
    An unrehearsed desire / Lauren B. Davis.

ISBN 978-1-55096-112-6

    I. Title.

PS8557.A8384U57 2008        C813'.6        C2008-905953-0

Design and Composition by Active Design Haus
Cover Photo by JupiterImages Corporation
Typeset in Stone Serif, Copperplate and Trajan fonts at the
    Moons of Jupiter Studios
Printed in Canada by Gauvin Imprimerie

The publisher would like to acknowledge the financial assistance of
the Canada Council for the Arts and the Ontario Arts Council, which is an
agency of the Government of Ontario.

Published in Canada in 2008 by Exile Editions Ltd.
144483 Southgate Road 14
General Delivery
Holstein, Ontario, N0G 2A0
info@exileeditions.com
www.ExileEditions.com

Canadian Sales Distribution:
McArthur & Company
c/o Harper Collins
1995 Markham Road
Toronto, ON M1B 5M8
toll free: 1 800 387 0117

# Contents

# IT COULD BE SERIOUS

The prickly sensation started in the back of Alice's throat, just a tickle really, a sort of hot, dry spot that swallowing didn't soothe. Oh, please, she thought, don't let me be getting sick again. Alice got sick frequently, not enough to be branded a weirdo like Arthur Spivak, a penicillin-smelling boy in her class who her mother said was "nearly translucent with illness," and whose pale temples were marbled with blue veins, but certainly Alice caught more than her fair share of colds and earaches and bouts of tonsillitis.

Alice was playing Mousetrap in Felicity Moreland's rec room. A room you were supposed to be allowed to wreck, Alice thought, whenever she heard the word, although of course that wasn't true at all. It was a dingy, chilly room with a grey, poured-concrete floor in the basement of the Moreland's three-bedroom red-brick bungalow. There were metal poles in the middle of the room that Alice assumed held up the house, and earlier Felicity had hung upside down from one of them and dared Alice to do the same, but she'd said no, because she was afraid of falling and cracking her head open. What an idiot she'd look like if that happened. Felicity now rolled the dice and moved her mouse. She collected a piece of cheese.

"Ha!" she said. "Your turn."

Alice landed on a dog bone space and so her turn was over. She clicked her tongue at the back of her mouth. It was sore, but not too sore. She decided to ignore it.

Felicity had two younger brothers and their belongings – GI Joes and hockey sticks, balls of various sizes, sports socks and mutilated toy soldiers – were strewn everywhere. The house smelled different than Alice's house. It smelled of slightly goatish, sweaty boys and fried food. When Alice went to the bathroom, she sniffed the pink towels and wrinkled her nose. Mildew. Sour milk. Perhaps this was what boys brought into a house. Alice herself was an only child, and how so many people got along in one space baffled her. Even when it was just Alice and her mother in their house, which was a split-level and larger than this house, it often seemed like there was no place to go to get away from each other. There was always a sense of the other, somewhere in the kitchen, or the bathroom, or down in the TV room.

Felicity landed on a build spot and added the rickety stairs to the mousetrap. Felicity and Alice were not the best of friends, not even good friends. Felicity belonged to a group of girls who played sports and always had dirty fingernails and scabs on their knees. They raced bicycles and built go-carts out of their old wagons and milk crates. They rollerskated wildly down the hill on Elm Street, howling and shrieking, with no thought to on-coming traffic. They disobeyed their parents and did not fear punishment.

Alice wasn't part of any particular group, although she very much wished this was not so. She longed to be part of a group, but it wasn't Felicity's group she coveted. Alice wanted to be part of the group of girls led by Kathy Baldwin and Carol McKay. These girls wore clothes not made by their mothers and not handed down by older sisters or cousins. They were so sure of themselves, with their shining hair and straight teeth. Pretty and popular and utterly unobtainable, they sat in a huddled group at the farthermost corner of the cafeteria, whispering, and laughing. And they played far more dangerous games than go-carts and field hockey, such as twirling around and around and around while holding their breath, and doing this until they passed out, sprawled on the grass with their legs apart and their eyes half closed, still and unselfconscious as if they were drugged. Sometimes they locked themselves in the girls' bathroom together and wouldn't let anyone else in. It was rumoured that they looked at each other's privates, and examined each other's chests for signs of breasts. They disobeyed their parents because they were sure of being able to squirm their way out of consequences. Boys became fools around them, cartwheeling, skateboarding, and showing off one minute, punching each other and cursing the next.

Life was like that – one group or the other, or none at all, like Alice, who sat during lunch by herself sometimes, or with other girls who weren't part of any group, but would never admit to being a group themselves. What would they be? The girls who nobody wanted? It was a peripheral life, as if they were the barnacles they learned about in science class, hanging onto the edge of things, hoping maybe someday the more attractive cluster would envelop them by the power of sheer proximity. Or chance. Or fate. Or there were days like today, when no one much seemed to be around, and so by default Alice and Felicity had floated together in the playground until, somewhat reluctantly, Felicity had invited Alice back to her place, to hang out, she said.

Felicity rummaged in the cardboard game lid. "I don't see it," she said.

"What?" said Alice.

"The stupid shoe that's supposed to tip the bucket that rolls the marble down the rickety stairs. I'll never trap the stupid mouse."

"Oh, well," said Alice.

"I hate living with boys," said Felicity.

Alice said she had to go to the bathroom.

"Again?" Felicity said.

In the bathroom, Alice swallowed and put her fingers on her throat under her jawbone. Little marble-sized swellings there. She opened her mouth wide and looked in the mirror. The light was at the wrong angle. She couldn't see if her throat looked sick. She felt awfully tired. She felt hollow inside.

When she went back downstairs, Felicity had turned the television on. *The Flying Nun*'s feet were just coming off the ground. "Dumb," said Felicity and she turned off the set. She asked Alice what she wanted to do now.

"I don't know," said Alice. "Maybe I should go." The truth was that her throat felt like it was full of razor blades, but she didn't want to tell Felicity, who played street hockey with her brothers and never wore shin guards and never complained about bruised shins and cuts and skinned knees.

Felicity shrugged.

Even the short walk from Felicity's house to Alice's took an enormous effort. The October wind sliced through her and she shivered. Her legs actually felt weak. Weak-kneed, jelly-legged, spaghetti-legs. She could have cried as she reached her driveway, and then the porch steps, and then the door knob. When she stepped inside the vestibule and called out to her mother that she was home, the air seemed suddenly too hot and her head spun. She smelled roasting meat, but the smell was flat, unappetizing, cloying. Her mother called out to her from the TV room in the basement. Voices from the television reached Alice, but they sounded funny, like someone playing with the volume control, turning it up and down, so that the sound came in waves.

She went up to her room and lay on the bed without taking off her coat or her shoes even. She just looked at the mauve walls, her mother's favourite colour. Alice's collection of stuffed animals and figurines decorated the white corner shelves, held up on the wall by metal brackets. The white horse her grandfather had brought her on his last trip reared up on its legs and you could see its private parts underneath. It was a very realistic horse, even if it was plastic. And the little mouse with a real kernel of corn between its paws, the hedgehog, the monkey, the German shepherd, the troll with the bright pink hair. It hurt her eyes to look at that hair. She swallowed. Shattered glass and turpentine.

The flannel pillowcase smelled so good, like lavender. It was sweet to lie there, almost like floating.

"What are you doing?" Her mother, Cynthia, stood in the doorway. Little pieces of thread and a tuft of pink fabric clung to her white blouse. She must have been sewing while she watched the television. "You've got mud on your shoes! You're dirtying the carpet!" Her mother's eyes snapped with disapproval. Floors in general were highly important to Alice's mother, and none more so than carpeted ones. Her mother was a small woman, barely five foot two, but she gave the impression of taking up a great deal of space. She was the sort of woman who claimed territory like an animal claims it, leaving mysterious scents and traces behind, so that it was clear to all passers-by that it was hers.

"I don't feel good," said Alice.

These were magic words, for Alice's mother was at her best in a health crisis. She put the back of her cool fingers against Alice's forehead. They smelled of Jergen's hand lotion.

"You have a fever. I'll get the thermometer. Get out of those clothes and into your pyjamas."

This was stern stuff, for it was only five o'clock. It was forbidden to appear at the dinner table in pyjamas. She was being sent to bed. Oh, she thought, I don't mind. And then she thought, I must be really sick.

Alice took off her clothes and meant to hang them up but then didn't; she simply put them on her dresser. Her mother would forgive her. Her mother would make an exception. Exceptions were one of the benefits of being sick.

She chose her blue flannel pyjamas, the ones with the flowers on them, the groovy ones, like the flowers Goldie Hawn had painted on her stomach on *Laugh In*.

When her mother came back, she said, "Let me look in your mouth," and tilted Alice's head towards the light so she could see inside. "Oh, dear," she said. "I don't like the look of your tongue."

"My tongue?"

"It doesn't look right at all. Does it hurt?"

"No. My throat hurts."

"I'll get you an aspirin. I don't like the looks of this." This was gratifying, as was the concern on her mother's face, altering her normally somewhat severe expression. "I don't think you'll be going to school tomorrow."

Alice nearly smiled. Staying home and having ice cream for lunch and watching *The Dick Van Dyke Show* and getting to read from *The Girl's Own Annual* – a special treat since it was an old and precious book her mother had had when she was just Alice's age – was a pretty good deal, as her father said. "You're getting a pretty good deal there," was what he said to anything he approved of, from the price of their new Ford Falcon, to those times when Alice was permitted to stay up past her bedtime to watch a special program on television. Which is when she remembered about tonight.

"What about *Daniel Boone?*" It was Thursday night. Her mother permitted her to stay up later, an entire half hour, to see Fess Parker as Daniel Boone.

Her mother shook the thermometer. "What about it? Open."

"Can I watch it?"

"We'll see."

While they waited for the thermometer to register the extent of Alice's illness, Cynthia picked up the discarded clothes, sorted them for wash or further wear, and put what was dirty in the clothes hamper in Alice's closet, and what was still clean she folded, and put away in the drawers. She polished away a smudge on the mirror with the cuff of her blouse. Alice's mother could never pass by a thing out of place. Kitchen cupboards left open were the undoing of her. "Why can't you close them when you've finished?" she'd say. "They look so messy." "If you pick things up as you go along," she'd say, "then you'll have half your work done for you." "You'll learn," she'd say. "When you're older. You have to conserve yourself." A woman of few friends and contempt for "joiners," as she called them, Alice's mother held the world at bay by swatting a dust cloth at it.

The thermometer clicked against Alice's teeth. Her mother removed it and frowned. "Oh dear," she said, and put her hand against her Alice's cheek. The fingers were hard and icy against Alice's flushed skin. "I'm going to get that aspirin."

When Alice's father came in from work, she heard her mother talking to him in the low voice she used for serious matters.

"I'm sure it's just another bout of tonsillitis," said her father.

More murmuring from her mother.

"You overreact," said her father.

"I do not overreact," said her mother. "You are under-involved."

"Don't start, Cynthia. I just got home."

"I suspect *you* started before you got here."

"Oh, come on now, don't be like that," said her father, and there was a moment's quiet, just the sound of someone being kissed. "I'm sure she's fine."

"We'll see," said her mother.

Her father came up to see her. He still wore his overcoat, and he brought with him the smell of oncoming snow and the metallic scent from inside the commuter train. "What's my girl up to?" he said.

"I'm sick."

"I can see that." He bent to kiss her and the odour of scotch and peppermints and tobacco floated on his breath. "Ah well, tomorrow's Friday, maybe you'll just stay home. How about that?"

"My throat hurts."

"Ice cream for dinner?"

"Sure. What about *Daniel Boone*?"

By seven-thirty, she was set up on the couch, in her mother's usual place, under a mound of blankets, with a big pillow under her head. If it wasn't for the pain in her throat, it would be a very good night. Her father sat in his chair, leafing through the paper. They never talked much in the evening. Her mother generally sat in the corner where Alice now sat, next to the good light and the side table, which was covered in an assortment of straight pins in two pin cushions, some with coloured heads, spools of thread, pinking shears, measuring tape, dress patterns in packages with drawings of the finished dresses on the front, a little hooked instrument that ripped out errant stitches, and an ivory nail buffer with a chamois skin that had been Alice's grand-mother's. The last time she had sat here, Alice had, for rea-sons mysterious even to her, cut a few things with scissors – the fringe on the sofa cover, some of the paper patterns, and lastly, and most inexplicably, a hunk of her own bangs. The latter she cut so short it looked as though something had taken a bite out of her hair. She got into a lot of trouble for that and her mother had hit her so hard with the hair brush that she broke the handle. When her teacher asked about the hairdo, Alice said her mother had done it.

Her father put down his paper. "Look at those rosy cheeks," he said. "Picture of health, right, kiddo?"

Alice smiled, but the truth was she did not feel anything like the picture of health. In fact, she wasn't completely sure she even cared much about Daniel Boone and his faithful Indian friend, Mingo. She knew, however, that it was impor-tant to her father that she not be too sick, or if she was, not to show it too much.

Alice's father, Andrew Cavanaugh Hastings, was a man who did not show pain. He had once fallen off a ladder that tipped as he leaned out too far from the roof while putting up Christmas lights. He lay on the ground for a moment, and then rose, brushed off his pant legs and said he was fine. It was not until four days later, when he was walking around all crinked over, that his wife had insisted he go to the doc-tor. Three broken ribs. When Alice had asked if it hurt, he'd said, "Only when I sneeze, so I'm not going to sneeze any more." And he'd winked at her. Mr. Hastings also suffered from ulcers, although he never spoke of it, and Alice and her mother only knew they were bothering him when he took to eating more ice cream than usual.

Alice's mother, on the other hand, made quite a drama of trauma, as her father said, using a phoney British accent to make it rhyme nicely. The traumas, though, were rarely Cynthia's. Cynthia could sniff out a neighbour's broken leg, or a dented fender, or a case of food poisoning, or a pending divorce with the acuity of a bloodhound. If she kept the world at bay and preferred to distance herself from the scrutiny of friends and relations, barricaded behind a wall of floor polish and fabric softener, she was downright avaricious when it came to other people's bad luck. She was delighted with any opportunity to get into someone else's house, under the pretext of delivering a tuna casserole or doing a little tidying up for someone under the weather, either emotional or physical, and was never happier than when she was caring for her own sick child. "You are my very own," she'd murmur, "my wee girl." And it was tempting to just lie beneath the milky kindness of those words, even if Alice did sometimes feel hurt when it seemed her mother was disappointed at her eventual recovery.

Her mother had gone off during a commercial break to consult the family medical encyclopedia on Alice's present condition. When she returned, she held the book out in front of her, open as an offertory, and she walked with the solemnity of a celebrant. Her face was serious, the eyes slightly wider than normal, the lips firm with courage and determination.

"What?" said her father.

"I think it could be serious," said her mother, and she transferred the weight of the book to one hand while the other went to her mouth.

"It's the flu," said her father.

"Look how red her face is. Alice," said her mother, coming toward her slowly, careful, as though she might bolt at any moment. "I need to see if you have a rash. It's all right. I just need to look."

Alice pulled down the blanket and, with slightly trembling fingers, her mother unbuttoned her pyjama top.

"Oh," said her mother. "Oh, Andrew."

There on Alice's chest was indeed a rash. It looked like sunburn. Her mother lifted her arm. In the crease, there were darker streaks. "Pastia's lines," said Cynthia, with something like awe in her voice. "I know what it is," she said.

"You're scaring the girl," said her father. "Stop it."

In fact, Alice was a little scared, but she was also excited, even through the haze of fever, where everything looked a little further away than it was.

"Look for yourself," said Cynthia. "Come and see." She sat beside Alice with her hands clasped and a look of suffering resignation on her face.

Slowly, with accompanying grunting protest, her father approached and looked. He frowned. "Let me see that book," he said, and then, when he had read what was on the page, "That can't be right. She's been inoculated, hasn't she?"

"Yes, but that doesn't mean she doesn't have it. Such things happen.

"I don't think so."

Cynthia's hands, still clasped, rose to just under her chin. "Scarlet fever," she whispered.

"I'm sure it isn't," said her father, and shut the book, rather more forcefully than necessary.

Andrew, however, was wrong. It was indeed scarlet fever. The next day Dr. Baldwin confirmed the diagnosis, adding that because Alice had indeed been inoculated, it wasn't as serious as it might otherwise have been. He prescribed antibiotics and bedrest.

"How long?" said Alice's mother.

"Oh, I'd say about a week before the infection's dealt with," said Dr. Baldwin. He sat down behind his tidy desk and polished his perfectly round shiny head. "Probably a few weeks before the tonsils and glands go completely down."

"A few weeks," repeated Cynthia.

And so Alice was kept home from school, and fed milkshakes with a raw egg in them to keep up her strength, and homemade soups and toast and ice cream and chamomile tea. She took aspirin and antibiotics and throat lozenges. These medicines she kept beside her bed on the turntable of her portable blue record player, like a Lazy-Susan cupboard. She twirled the bottles around and around, the orange aspirins in their brown bottle, the bright yellow lozenges, the mentholated rub in the lovely blue jar to soothe her chest, even though she didn't have a cough, and the bottle of mauve-ish liquid antibiotic that tasted so foul. Her mother gave her a green grape after each swallow of antibiotic, to wash the taste away. Alice read books like *The Lion, the Witch and the Wardrobe,* and an assortment of Nancy Drew novels. She watched *Andy of Mayberry* in the mornings, and in the afternoons she and her mother watched the matinee movie on channel twelve. She dozed while her mother watched *Another World.*

It was so nice, just her and her mother, passing the days like this. In the evenings, when her father came home from work and came to see her, she liked the way the visit felt formal. She imagined she was a little girl from Victorian times, like the pale heroine of a novel, or like little Colin from *The Secret Garden.* Her father sat by her bed and asked her how she was feeling. The first few days she said she was feeling pretty good and he said that was wonderful and gave her something he'd brought for her – a chocolate bar, or a pack of gum, or a necklace made from candy. If she was allowed to go downstairs and watch television in the evening for an hour or two, cuddled up under the blankets, her father gave her a piggyback to bed, even though she was rather too old for such a thing. Sickness made it possible, her frailty, as her mother called it.

On the fifth day, he asked how she was feeling, and she said "Not very much better, I'm afraid."

"Oh?" said her father. "What's the matter?"

"Well, I'm sick."

"I know that. But why is it worse?" He looked annoyed, which is how he often looked if he was worried.

"I don't know. Perhaps I'll have a relapse," she said.

"You heard that from your mother," her father said. "Did your teacher send you homework so you don't fall behind?"

"I don't think so," Alice said, and she hoped not, because she would much rather read *A Wrinkle in Time* than study arithmetic any day.

"We'll see about that," said her father.

Later, she heard her parents arguing and she knew it was about her, but that didn't seem like such a bad thing, to be at the centre like this.

The one disappointment was that no one came to visit her, but her mother assured her they would have if they could, but she was simply far too contagious and they did not want to put other children at risk, now did they?

"But did anyone deliver homework?" she said.

"You're such a silly girl. Why would you want to work when you should be working on nothing more than getting better? Besides, you're so smart, you'll catch up in no time, when you go back to school."

That made sense, for she was smart. Alice decided it was perfectly all right to give her energies over to getting better. That should be her focus, as her mother said. So, in between reading and television and snacks, she took naps and lay in bed watching the golden flutter of autumn leaves from the giant oak outside her window. She imagined she was in a glass snowflake globe, floating in a thick, glossy sea, with gold flakes falling around her.

One night, when he father had carried her up to bed and tucked her in, he said, "Really, Peaches, how are you feeling?"

"Well, I don't have much strength," she said.

Her father sighed. He took her hand and held it firmly, patting it over and over. "Listen to me," he said. "You have to fight, do you understand? You have to fight this thing."

"It takes weeks," said Alice.

"Punch it in the nose, kiddo," said her father, and then he left, closing the door softly behind him.

Alice lay in the dark, wondering what he was talking about. She thought he should be more sympathetic, really.

It was more than three weeks by the end of the illness. Nearly a month, she thought, when she woke one morning. *I have been a true invalid.* Then she thought, well, maybe just a little longer, and called her mother for some toast and tea.

At last, the day came when all the medicine was finished and her glands were down to normal and she was, to tell the truth, just a tiny bit restless. It was a Saturday afternoon and the sun was bright, even if the air was chilly. From the back-yards, the voices of her schoolmates rose and fell in the melody of their game. There were no fences around any of the houses and the grassy squares became one long play-ground. Swing sets behind one house, jungle gym behind another, a tether-ball pole, a basketball net, and in between the rolling, leaf-scattered grass to leap about in, to roll in, to chase each other through. She heard Felicity's voice, and maybe Carol's. The sounds were a little foreign, but beckoning, full of resonance.

Alice sat at the kitchen table across from her father. He read the sports section, she read the funnies and did the word games. He lowered the paper and she noticed he hadn't shaved this morning. "Sounds like a pack of coyotes out there," he said.

"It's a terrible noise," said her mother, who was at the stove browning meat for tonight's stew. The kitchen smelled of oregano and fat and pepper.

"Alice's friends," Andrew said.

"Oh, I don't think that's her crowd," said Cynthia.

"I know them. I think that's Felicity."

"Why don't you go see?" said her father. "You've been cooped-up in here far too long."

"I don't think that's a good idea, Drew. She's still convalescing."

"I, I think I might like to."

"Don't feel pressured just because your father says things."

"Cynthia, she looks like a little ghost. She needs some sun. A good run round will do her the world of good."

"I'm going to go out. Just for a little while," said Alice.

"I was going to make you some cinnamon toast," said her mother. "And some tea."

The voices were louder now and she could practically smell the sunshine. Her feet tingled. "I won't be out for long and I can have it when I come back."

"Well . . ."

"Please, please?"

"Go on, Alice. Go on," said her father.

She was up and out of her chair in a flash. Quicker, really, than she'd thought possible. Suddenly she wanted movement, wanted to flex things. She twitched with it.

"Are you sure you're up to it? Wear your jacket and scarf," Cynthia called.

Alice rounded the corner of the house and caught sight of them – red and blue and green coats flashing against the dark leaf-tattered tree trunks at the back of the MacKay's house, where the street, and the yards, dead-ended into forest.

"Hey," she called but, of course, they couldn't hear her. "It's me, Alice."

She set out at a trot, but in less than a minute she was winded, her legs tired. She wondered if maybe her mother was right, perhaps she wasn't ready to be out yet, but her heart clenched at the thought of missing Kathy and Carol and even Felicity, whose voice she could clearly hear, louder than the rest, yelling out from between the trees. Things would be different now, she was sure. They would be interested in her since she had suffered this Terrible Illness, and come through it so bravely.

The air was rich with the scent of autumn, of burning leaves and the crisp freshness that foretells oncoming winter. It gave her energy and she walked a little, and ran a little, until she reached the edge of the woods.

"Hey," she called.

The girls were by the streambed, which was low at this time of year. It was dappled with fallen leaves, gold and red against the slate-grey water and the stones. It was Kathy in the red coat, Carol in the blue. They looked like two painted boulders, hunkered down by the edge of the water. Felicity and the other girls were farther along into the woods, whooping and running, chasing each other with sticks.

"Hi," said Alice again.

Kathy looked over her shoulder and nudged Carol. "Look who it is," she said.

"What are you doing out?" said Carol. She brushed her long hair back over her shoulder, tucking it back behind her ear.

"I'm all better."

"No," said Kathy.

The two girls stood up. Kathy was taller than Carol, but both their noses were perfectly pert and their teeth were straight. Kathy had red hair, as wavy as Carol's was silken and straight. Even Kathy's freckles were perfect.

"What are you doing?" said Alice. She smiled with every muscle in her face. She wanted to beam at them, to glow with them. She wondered what she had been doing in the house with her mother all these weeks, when here, right at the end of her street was this magic forest of possibilities. She felt like an elf, maybe, yes – like the three of them, even Felicity and the wild girls, were fairies in this wood, and that anything could happen.

"You can't be around us," said Carol, and she linked her arm through Kathy's.

"What?" The smile on Alice's face was heavy then, and so she let it droop. "Why?"

"Because you carry germs." Carol giggled.

"Typhoid Mary, that's what my mother calls you," and Kathy giggled as well. "It means that you aren't safe to be around."

The other girls, the wild girls, had stopped their whooping and hollering and come closer. Alice looked over her shoulder. They formed an unsmiling half-circle behind her.

"I don't carry germs. I'm better," said Alice.

"We don't want you here," said Felicity, coming forward. She had a smear on her cheek and it looked like war paint to Alice. "I'm lucky I didn't die, being around you, letting you in my house."

"That's stupid." This wasn't what was supposed to happen at all. Alice's lower lip began to tremble. She imagined the conversations that had gone on at school these last three weeks. The whispering between Carol and Kathy.

Kathy took a few steps forward. "Go home, Alice. No one wants you around."

"No."

"I mean it, go home." Kathy's face flushed. She folded her arms across her chest and glared.

"I threw your homework in the garbage," said Carol, and Alice could not believe how proud of herself she sounded. "As if I'd bring it to your house! My mother said if Mrs. Sergeant wanted you to get your homework she could jolly well bring it to you herself."

It was strange, and frightening, the way the other girls had gone quiet, as if they were waiting for something to happen, as if they were waiting to pounce. Alice's heart was a rabbit in her chest, scrunched down and frozen, beating at twelve times normal.

"You'll fail this year, you've missed so much. You'll get held back and we won't have to have you in our class again."

A gust of wind swirled through the trees, and all around them, the golden leaves fluttered and danced. One struck Alice in the face and stuck there. It was cold and a little sharp. She brushed if off while the girls laughed. She would not cry, no matter what they said, she vowed she would not cry. She looked down at her mud-covered shoes. She had stepped into a boggy patch without noticing.

Someone poked her between the shoulder blades. She spun around. Felicity had come up behind her and now pointed her finger. "Scram," she said.

Alice took a couple of steps back. She hadn't meant to, she just did, out of shock. Were they actually going to beat her up, like boys? She turned around again, frightened now, of being surrounded. Carol, in her coat as blue as the coldest ice, stepped forward. She pushed Alice in the chest with both hands.

She had been so excited to see them. So pleased. So hopeful.

She'd been such an idiot, thinking they'd be happy to see her. When were they ever truly happy to see her? So smug in their stupid little groups.

Before Alice realized she was going to do it, she grabbed a hank of Carol's hair. She wrapped it around in her fist and yanked. Carol screamed. The hair felt cool and soft, and so slippery Alice really had to mangle her fingers through it to keep hold. Her stomach churned and her skin was hot with a different sort of fever than the one she'd had before. Carol dug her fingernails into the back of Alice's hand and yelled for her to let go. It was odd, how quiet the world had gone. Alice was surprised she was doing this. Carol's fingernails hurt, but it didn't matter. It made no difference whatsoever. In a detached sort of way, from behind the wall of her fury, she wondered what would happen. The only thing she knew for sure was that she was not going to let go of Carol's hair until it came out of her head in a hunk. Kathy simply stood there with her mouth open. Carol looked so deeply surprised.

"Hey!" said Felicity, behind her. And then, "Whoa!" with something very close to admiration.

In Alice's head, she heard her father's words. *Fight this thing. Punch it in the nose, kiddo.* She tightened her grip. She had never felt stronger.

# DIRTY MONEY

It happened last summer, a season I call The Time of the Naked Guys. Of course, I was ten then and didn't know as much as I do now. It was a real hot summer, and the air around town smelled of baking asphalt during the day and barbeques at night, since none of the mothers wanted to cook much. This one afternoon I was sitting on the porch eating a blue Popsicle, which is my favourite colour Popsicle although it doesn't really taste like anything blue, but then what does? Blueberries, I guess, but Popsicles don't taste like that. Anyway, a white van pulled up in front of our driveway and the man driving asked me to come over.

"Hey, kid" he called, as he leaned over and rolled down the passenger side window. "I'm looking for the public swimming pool." He was alone.

"You're on the wrong road," I said, going over to the van. "You got to go back and down Biscayne to Castle Road. This is a dead end."

"You think they'll mind if I don't wear a bathing suit?" He moved his hand in his lap.

That was when I realized he had his pants unzipped and his *thing* was all big and purple-y in his hand. It was as if I'd just dived into cold water.

"You'll have to ask them," I said, which at the time I thought was a cool, un-freaked out thing to say. It was the first *thing* I'd ever seen, since I don't have any brothers or cousins or anything and I wouldn't of minded taking a longer look, but it scared me. I hightailed it back in the house to tell my mom.

I came into the kitchen opening and closing my mouth like a fish. When I finally sputtered out what had happened, I figured she'd phone the police or *something*. Like the week before when the same thing happened to Janet Drury, and her father and brother chased the car all the way down the street, her father waving a rake around like a sword.

"What are you talking about?" my mom said. Her hands were sticky with marshmallows from the Rice Crispy squares she was making, and her permed hair had gone frizzy in the heat.

"Some guy! You know, with his *thing* out," I said.

"Sweet Jesus! You shouldn't be going near strange men," she said.

I ground a lost kernel of puffed rice under my foot until it was nothing but dust on the black and white linoleum. The way Mom looked at me, I felt like I was the one who'd been out there with my God-givens bouncing around for the whole world to see.

"Why can't you stay in the playground and play with the other kids? I blame your aunt for this. The way you run wild in the woods all the time." I watched the skin under my mother's arm flap back and forth as she stirred the thickening goo.

"You're ten years old, Kathy, very nearly a young lady. You're far too old to be running wild the way you do. You're just asking for trouble. He didn't touch you, did he?"

"'Course not," I said.

"Well, good then. And take your hair out of your mouth; you look like a little idiot."

I have long straight mouse-brown hair and chewing on it is a bad habit I've had since I was a little kid. I pulled it out of my mouth.

"I don't know what the world's coming to," Mom said. "It's not like we live in the city, with all those Eye-talians and J-e-w-s." Mom always spelled out anything she didn't think was fit to say outright. I waited for her to say or do something more, but that seemed to be her final word on the subject. She wasn't a "making-a-fuss" kind of mom, not one to get into a "tizzy," as she called it, about trouble. Although my experience was it was only *my* trouble she didn't get bothered about. She sure was prone to pitching hissy-fits when it came to stuff she personally didn't like.

I went out onto the porch and sat down on the steps. The boards were so hot they near burnt up the back of my thighs.

"You stay outta those woods, Kathy, you hear me? I want you to promise me."

"Yes, ma'am," I said, although I couldn't see the sense in it. I hadn't been in the woods. The naked man had practically driven right up to our own house, after all. Sometimes the way grown-ups think is a bafflement to me. I was suspicious that Mom wasn't mad about the man at all, but as usual, was mad about Aunt Shirley and getting things all tangled up in her mind.

It was Aunt Shirley, my dad's sister, who taught me the magic of the woods, although if my Mom and Dad knew, they'd skin me alive and boil Aunt Shirley in oil. They already figured she was half-crazy, but she's not. She knows stuff. And she's a wood-walker, just like me.

I've always been drawn out into the woods like under some enchantment. In the field past the stone wall, the first stand of birch trees and the big oak, is my special place: an abandoned apple orchard with a stream running through it that isn't much more than a trickle in August, but runs like a chorus of glory in the springtime. The trees are all ramble-down and scrabble, pretty much forgotten by everybody.

Except me and Aunt Shirley, that is.

Aunt Shirley came down and spent three weeks with us every summer. Mom didn't like it much and didn't put flowers in her room like she did when her own sister came to visit. For me, though, it was the best time of the year.

We went walking out in the woods early every morning she was there. Sometimes she'd come and get me before the house was even awake. She put her fingers against my lips to rouse me quietly and we snuck down the narrow stairs in the dusty shimmers of first light, being careful of the creaky third step. It was our private ritual, she said. We went out across the back field and over the stone fence, which was slick with moss and dew. Our feet got wet and we shivered against the chill, but stood it, knowing we'd be warm as soon as the sun was full up in the sky. She showed me plants that made medicine.

"The forests and meadows are God's drugstore, Kat," she said. "A living, breathing pharmacy."

We picked stuff like five-finger grass, which is good for loose bowels; yarrow, which cleans the blood and treats the piles; blue cohosh for women's cramps, and black snakeroot for bad skin and nervousness. Aunt Shirley gathered the plants in her sweetgrass basket that had been woven by a special friend. Then we'd go to the stand of cedars near the stream and she'd put her basket down and raise her hands up to the light.

"You must always breathe in beauty, walk in beauty, dance in beauty," she'd say. She twirled around in slow circles with her robin's-egg blue shawl that came all the way from Spain and her black hair swirling around her. I thought Aunt Shirley was the most beautiful woman in the world.

"There is magic all around," she said, holding my face in her cool hands, my nostrils filling up with her smell of vanilla and something deep and woody. "Close your eyes and repeat after me: God is alive. Magic is afoot. God is alive. Magic is afoot."

We repeated the words over and over until they became a chant and then a song and then nothing but sound rising in the air. She caught my hands in hers and we spun around and around and fell back on the soft mossy earth, the sky reeling, and our eyes wet from laughing.

She taught me it was places like this, under the protection of the trees and sky, which were most sacred to God.

"Church is all right as far as it goes," she said, "and I suppose that's pretty far for some, but for me, this is where the Spirit lives." Her eyes were bright as black stones on a sun-dazzled river bottom. "Can't you just feel it?"

I was sure I could.

Mornings were for Aunt Shirley and me, and magic.

"You're just like your Aunt Shirley," Mom would say and mean it not in a good way. "You be careful you don't end up like her, too." By which she meant living in a railway caboose sixty miles north of Scout's Landing on Blue Bird Lake, near the Red Dog Indian Reservation.

"She lets Indians sit at her *table*," she'd whisper and shake her head.

I remember one day Mom and her friend Sylvia were sitting around smoking cigarettes and picking at a cinnamon coffee cake.

"A woman alone like that, well," Mom said, "you can *imagine*." She made her eyes as wide as possible and raised her eyebrows. She pulled her chin to her chest and three rolls of fat puffed out her neck. "I'd be very interested to know how she makes ends meet, if you catch my meaning."

I was moused-up in a corner stool in the kitchen, under the African violets that crowded the windowsill. I ate spoonfuls of chocolate milk powder from the tin and tried to stay quiet enough so they'd forget I was listening.

"A touch of the tar brush there, I suspect," she said. "You know, she's only Bob's half-sister. Some say their mother was, how shall I put this nicely, *friendly* with . . ." and she leaned over to Sylvia's waiting ear and whispered something.

"No!" said Sylvia, her eyes wide as an owl.

"It's what they say," said Mom, nodding wisely, her finger against the side of her beaky nose.

I'd never heard that "tar brush" expression before. I got my behind smacked smart later for asking Dad what it meant.

"It just means that whereas all the rest of the family's fair, your Aunt Shirley's got olive skin and black hair and brown eyes. That's *all* it means, you understand?" said Dad. "Do you?"

"Yes, sir," I said, rubbing my stinging backside and feeling the injustice of the world. "I just asked."

"Well, don't" he said, and huffed off to find Mom.

Then came the day of the third naked man, the one down in the orchard. It was one of those days when even though the sky's clear as the chlorine-shocked public pool, there's a crackle of something in the air. You wake up just knowing everybody's going to be snappish and if something nasty has been waiting to happen, it's going to happen today. And, sure enough, it wasn't but lunch when all hell broke loose.

My mom and dad and Aunt Shirley had a whopper of a fight. The kind where I was thrown out of the house for the duration. Aunt Shirley'd been kinda sick on and off her whole visit, so sick a couple of days that we'd missed our wood walks. I thought it was mean as hell, my mother picking on her the way she did, and Mom chose a day when she was particularly under the weather to start the fight.

"You'd best go out and play for a time, Kathy. I need to have a few words with *her*," Mom'd said jerking her neck in the direction of the bathroom where sounds of Aunt Shirley being sick could be heard.

"I want to stay and make sure she's all right."

"No. Out. Now." She pointed to the door.

"D-a-a-d," I pleaded.

"Go pick some berries or something," he said, his stubby hands pushed way deep into the pockets of his jeans, his fingers rattling all his coins, which was never a good sign.

"Fine," I said, as unhappily as I could, and grabbed the aluminium berry-pail from beside the sink.

I stood next to the side door of our house, pressed up against the prickly green stucco, trying to hear what was going on. After a few minutes, Aunt Shirley came out of the bathroom. My mom was waiting for her. At first, I couldn't make out what they were saying, but their voices started to rise as they moved into the kitchen.

"You are a woman completely without shame!" my mother yelled.

"I have nothing to be ashamed of, Libby," said Aunt Shirley.

"How can you say that? It's indecent! It's obscene!"

"Don't get yourself all worked up now, Lib," said my dad.

"Worked *up*? I'll give you worked up! You haven't seen worked up!"

"This really doesn't concern you, now does it?" said Aunt Shirley. Her voice was as calm as always, the sound of a cool river breeze on a sweltering day.

"It certainly does concern me, as long as you insist on presenting yourself at my door, expecting to be taken in whenever you darn well feel like it. It concerns me as long as you keep trying to insinuate yourself into the affections of my only daughter!"

My ears were burning for sure now. I held my breath.

"Indians!" my mother yelled, as though a bunch of wild red men were coming in through the back window. "Indians! My God."

"Not 'Indians,' Libby. Indian. His name is Daniel Migwins."

"More likely the whole tribe on a bargain rate!"

"Libby, keep quiet a minute!" said my dad. "I suppose you're going to want to marry this guy?" Even though I couldn't see him, I could tell by the tone of his voice that he was glowering something awful and was probably pulling at his ear the way he did when he was real mad.

"No, I don't know if I do or not. We haven't decided."

"That is *it*!" Mom's voice rose way up to a squeak. "The last straw. You are not welcome here any longer, Shirley MacDonald. I will not have you around Kathy. You will leave my house."

"Is that what you want too, Doug?" Aunt Shirley's voice was so low I could barely hear it.

"It might be for the best. At least for a while."

"I see."

"I hope to heaven that you do!" said Mom.

"A fine mess you've made, Shirley. Jesus! I need some air," said Dad. His footsteps sounded on the linoleum floor and I dashed around the corner of the house and along the path to the berry patch. My heart pounded like a jackhammer.

I knew I better stay away for a while. So, I filled the pail halfway with berries. But all the time my mind was whirling with the information I'd heard.

When I went back to the house Dad told me I'd better head off for the afternoon. Let things cool down a little.

"Is Aunt Shirley going away?" I said.

"I don't know, Kitten, I don't know." He ran his fingers through his thin hair. "Don't you worry about it though, all right? Just go play some place for a few hours. Things'll be better by dinner time. We'll be all right."

"What'd she do?"

He turned me round and gave me a gentle push.

"You ask too many questions. Git!"

So me and Ginny, who's my best friend, went climbing trees near the stream in my orchard. We were sitting up high, peeling the bark off the dead branches and looking for the secret writing left on the smooth wood by worms, the trails and snaky lines we knew meant something mysterious. Secret Indian writing, maybe. Ginny was a branch lower than me. She had trouble climbing because she was chubby and her shorts were always too tight. She said she was afraid they'd split if she had to reach her legs too far. Ginny had long wheaty hair in a thick braid down her back. She said it weighed a ton and she wanted to cut it off but her mother wouldn't let her because she said it was her best feature. I envied that hair.

Ginny dropped her head back and shrugged her shoulders to get the weight of the braid off her neck. Then she grabbed me by the arm, pinching me.

"Ow!" I yelled. Her eyes were wide behind her thick pink-framed glasses.

"Kathy, look!" She pointed to the other side of the stream. I looked but didn't see anything.

"Look," she said again, "there, next to the rocks."

"What're you looking at?" I strained to see. "What is that?"

"I think it's a man."

I could make out a shape in the long dry grass.

"It's a dog or a coyote or something."

"That's no dog!"

"Yeah, you're right. Wait a minute! I don't think he's got any clothes on."

"Not a stitch," she whispered. "We should get out of here."

"*He* should get out of here," I said. It made me mad, seeing him there. How did he even find his way here? This was not a place most people even knew about. My blood was boiling to think of this man, this *naked* man in my special place. "He's got no business here."

"It's not your orchard."

"I claimed it. I'm the only one who comes here. You only come here because I bring you."

"I'm going." She started to climb down the tree.

"Go then, if you want." I broke a piece of dead branch off and chucked it across the stream. It landed with a soft flop on the far bank.

"Kathy! Don't!"

"Hey, you! Get out of here! You're trespassing!" I yelled.

The man sat up and looked in our direction. My heart started to beat fast, but I held on tight to the wood even though my palms were slippery. He looked hard at the tree. He had a big head, full of black hair and his eyes were small.

"Now you've done it," said Ginny, "he's seen us sure."

"So?" I said, trying to sound brave.

For a second I could have sworn he was looking straight in my eyes. He held his hand up to keep the sun out. He wore a thick silver chain bracelet around his wrist. He was smiling and his teeth were very white. I scrambled down as fast as I could put hand over hand. I scratched my ankle on a patch of rough bark and skinned my shin. The blood soaked through my cotton socks in a bright round spot.

Ginny and I huddled at the base of the tree.

"You think he'll just leave?" I said.

"I don't know."

"Maybe we should go, too."

"Look and see what he's doing," said Ginny.

"You look," I said.

"No, you're the one that threw stuff at him – you look."

"Chicken!" I said, and slowly stood up. I couldn't see him anywhere. I ducked down again.

"I think he's gone," I said.

"You shouldn't have done that, Kathy. Thrown that stick at him."

"Scared him off, didn't I?"

Ginny stood, and tugged the legs of her blue shorts down over her round bottom.

"I'm going home."

"Hi, there," a voice said. We near jumped out of our skins.

Sure enough, there was the naked man. Except he was not naked any more. His black shoes were all muddy, so I figured he must have jumped the stream and slid a bit. He had on beige pants with dirt spackles around the cuffs and a black belt, a red-and-brown plaid shirt with a tear at the pocket. He'd missed a belt loop on his pants and the waist sat funny, drooping a bit. He carried a ring of keys in his hand.

"My name's Cliff," he said. "Didn't know anybody came out here. Thought I was alone. What're your names?"

"Kat," I said, and crossed my arms in front of me. Ginny slapped my arm.

"Like kitty-cat. That's a cute name." When he smiled his teeth looked too big for his mouth, like big horse teeth.

"It's Kathy."

"I like Cat better, don't you?" He looked at Ginny. "And what about you, don't you have a name?"

"Yeah."

"Don't want to tell me, huh?"

"I'm not supposed to talk to strangers."

"You think I'm strange?"

"I don't know." She shuffled her feet at the tree roots.

"Well, I'm not. Just somebody who enjoys being out in nature, like you." He spread his arms wide and breathed deep. "Sure is a pretty day. You kids come out here often?"

"This is my place," I said.

"Is it? Well, I don't mean to trespass. Didn't know it was anyone's place in particular. Hope you'll accept my apologies."

"Yeah," I said.

"Thing is, I'd move along, except I've got a problem."

"What kinda problem?" said Ginny, who was holding onto the end of her braid and tugging on it as though she were trying to pull herself free.

"See, I've been out walking around in these woods for a while now. Just enjoying the day, the woods, you understand. And it seems that I've dropped my wallet – some place between here and the main road. I looked all around down where you saw me sitting. But I can't find it anywhere. I'm sure I dropped it climbing over some of the stone fences out there." He pointed in a general sort of way, towards the woods to the west.

"I'd be ever so grateful if you girls could help me find it. I've got some photos in there of my own little girl, about your age. I'd hate to lose that. And of course, I got some money in there, too. In fact, I'd be pleased to reward you both if you found it for me. I'd pay you a dollar a piece."

"I don't think so," said Ginny.

"Silver dollars. I got a couple of 'em in my wallet."

"Did you come on the old track by the silo?" I asked, looking in the wrong direction.

"Through that way. Yes," he said.

Now, I knew those woods better than anybody alive, I bet. Knew every place to duck, run, or hide. This man thought he was so smart. I could show him.

"Kathy . . ." Ginny warned, "I want to go home."

"Then go ahead," I said, knowing she would not go home alone, not with this man around. "Come on, mister. Follow me." I started off at a trot, giving him a wide berth and headed across the field to the rocks that crossed the stream.

"Kathy!"

"Come on, Ginny." And because the only choice she had was to stay with the man or come with me, she ran with me. I felt a little mean about it, knowing Ginny was scared.

"Don't be afraid," I said when she caught up. "We're gonna really show this guy the woods, okay?"

"You're going to get us in trouble!"

"Naw."

"Hey, wait up," called the man, hurrying after us.

We headed into the forest and scrambled over the first stone wall, then scrabbled down the ravine. We ran so quick the sun through the trees went dark-light-dark-light and made us feel like we were blinking our eyes real fast.

"I don't think I came this way," he called.

"It's a short cut," I called back. Ginny giggled.

At the bottom of the ravine, we crossed the fallen log to the other side and started up the steep bank. I heard the man start across the log and then slip, cussing as he got a soaker full of muck on the soft bottom. At the top of the ravine bank, we made a quick dash across the meadow and into the edge of the cedars.

"Hey!" the man called again.

"Hurry up," I called.

"You're going too fast to look for my wallet."

"No, I'm looking real good. Aren't you, Ginny?"

"Yeah, real good!"

"Wait for me," he said.

We went on deeper into the forest, kept turning, and shouting for him to follow. We dodged and dipped around for about fifteen minutes. We kept a good ways ahead of him, which was easy, slow and klutzy as he was. He stumbled and rooted around like a hog.

"This way," said Ginny, and she looped around the patch of stinging nettle we'd fallen prey to ourselves a couple of weeks before. She stood in the middle of the path on the other side, waving back at our companion. He headed right for the nettle.

"Goddamn it! Goddamn it!"

We took off fast, ducked down through the old barbed-wire fence, and kept going, farther into the cool dark, where all the fallen fir needles were soft sponge on the forest floor. The clean scent of pine and cedar made our noses tingle but when our feet landed hard the smell of mushrooms and rot rose from the ground. Behind us, we heard him say words we weren't allowed to say.

He slipped and almost fell to his knees.

"That's it. I'm heading back," he called and turned.

"Not that way, mister. That's the wrong way. You'll get lost for sure," I said. "You want to go back, we'll take you."

He turned around in circles, trying to get his bearings, but it was no good.

"Damn it! All right, then. Just get me out of here."

"What about your wallet?" I said.

"To hell with my wallet!"

"Okay, then."

"You're crazy," said Ginny. Her face was all shiny and her hair damp on her forehead, but she was laughing.

We crossed a stand of birches, climbed over another stone fence and hopped across a small stream. Then we stood waiting for him. He was breathing hard and his face was red as a beet.

"Don't need to cross that, mister. You're back."

He looked around and put his hands up to his head. He groaned.

"This is where we started. You took me around in a circle."

He was panting. Big dark wet patches stained the underarms of his shirt. He bent over, hands on his knees. A bead of sweat fell from the end of his nose.

"Sorry, mister. Guess you lost your wallet for good," I said.

"We gotta go," said Ginny.

"Well, I'll be damned," the man puffed. "Look at this."

"What?" I said, not getting any closer.

"My wallet, right here. Must have dropped it when I was sitting here."

"Must have."

"You sure are lucky," said Ginny. "I thought it was a goner."

He bent down and picked it up. Brushed it off and went to put it in his back pocket.

"Hey," I said. "You said you'd give us a dollar if we found it."

"But I found it."

"We helped. You wouldn't have come back here if it wasn't for us."

The man looked at me a minute, his eyes clouding over with something filmy and mean. Then all at once, he threw back his head and laughed a big rough craggle of sound. Ginny jumped.

"I'll be pissed," he said, "I'll be pissed."

He wiped his eyes and put his wallet in his back pocket.

"I seem to be out of silver dollars."

"That's okay, we'll take paper."

"You're a tough little kid, you know that?"

"I guess."

"I don't think I like tough little girls." He reached in his pocket and dug out a handful of change. "This do?"

"It will if it's two dollars."

He held out his hand. "Take it."

"I'd prefer if you put it on that rock, mister."

He grinned his muley grin and put the change on the rock.

Then he turned, quick as a cat, his arms wide flung and yelled "RAAAAAGH!"

I thought my heart was going to jump out of my throat and Ginny grabbed my arm. Even with the stream between us, we turned tail and ran a few paces. Then I glanced over my shoulder.

The man was laughing, and walking away. Waving his hand like he knew we'd look.

Ginny was crying. "I want to go home, Kathy, I want to go home."

"Okay. But first I'm going to get that money."

I waited till he'd moved off a good long way, then I ran fast as I could, grabbed the coins and headed off at a run, Ginny beside me, snuffling away. When we got back to the stone wall that separated the fields from our backyards, we stopped to count it.

"There's almost three dollars here!" I said. It was a sweaty little pile of treasure in my palm.

"Wow." Ginny touched it with the tip of her finger and then quickly pulled her hand away and put it behind her back. "What are we going to do with it?"

"You keep it."

"Really? Me?"

"Yeah. Don't spend it." I held out the money and dropped it into her hand, one coin at a time. "We'll make a pact." We twisted our pinkie fingers together. "We'll do something real great with it. We'll buy stuff and build a tree house in the orchard, maybe. Or what else? What do you want to do with it?"

"I was thinking about a hamster," she said.

"Well, sure. We'll have enough for that, too."

We walked along, planning out our purchases, until, longing for the cool sweet taste of cherry Kool-Aid, I headed back to my house. Since my mom wasn't a whole lot of help with the pervert in the car, I didn't figure I'd tell her about this guy, especially since I knew the way she felt about me hanging around in the woods.

"Where's Aunt Shirley?" I said.

"In her room."

"She sick?"

"Sick, eh?" Mom looked at me with a funny expression. Then she went back to the dishes she was washing. "Yeah, sure, she's *sick*."

"Can I go up and see her?"

"No."

"Why not?"

"Because I said so. Now get out of my hair! There must be something in the air," she muttered. "Everybody's gone crazy. Skeedaddle!" She waved a soapy brush at me.

I was lying in bed that night, trying not to think too much about Aunt Shirley. It was obvious something was really wrong and wasn't going to get any better any time soon. All through dinner the adults had been quiet as coffins, not talking to each other and not talking to me much either. It made it hard to swallow, even the soft stuff like mashed potatoes and creamed corn. Aunt Shirley smiled at me a time or two, but I could tell she was real upset. She gave me a hug and went up to bed right after dinner.

I lay there, watching the North Star through the branches of the oak in the backyard and tried to keep my mind off things by figuring out what I was going to do with my new-found wealth. After a while my parents came up to bed. They talked softly, their voices just a hum through the wall. A few minutes later, my mother's voice rose up and I could make out the words.

"So that's how she's been supporting herself all these years." My mother's voice clanged. "I thought as much. Filthy money from those men! Dirty money!"

"You're letting your imagination run away with you." Dad sounded tired and sad.

"Good riddance, I say!"

"Keep your voice down, Libby."

It took me a long time to get to sleep.

Aunt Shirley came to my room real early next morning. Mother-of-pearl combs held her hair in a messy pile on the top of her head. She had bluish-grey smudges under her eyes. She told me she was leaving.

"But why?"

"That's the way it has to be for a while."

"But *why*?"

She took my hand and put it on her stomach. "Things change, Kat, that's part of the magic. It comes from the most unlikely places."

"I don't understand."

"You will," she smiled.

"I don't want you to go," I said.

"I wish I didn't have to go."

"I could come with you."

"No, Sweetie, your place is here. When you're older, you can come visit me. In the meantime, you remember everything I taught you, won't you?"

"I'll remember," I said, but it was hard to talk.

She put her arms around me and hugged me tight.

In the morning, she was gone. And nobody would tell me what was going on. It was as if she'd never been there and I wasn't allowed to talk about it.

"But what *happened?*" I wailed.

"Nothing happened," said my mother. "And that's all there is to it." She clamped her mouth down in that firm line I knew permitted no discussion. "Absolutely nothing happened here."

I took a little paprika bottle from the drawer, emptied out the paprika in the back garden, where I figured it would kill slugs, and then went to St. Anne's Church. I slipped in the big wood doors, and made for the stone bowl in the chapel. I scooped a bit of church water into the empty bottle and headed over to Ginny's.

When she showed up at the door I told her to get the money.

"We have to bury it," I said. "We can't spend it."

"Why not?" said Ginny. "I want to go down to Dougall's and buy a goldfish."

"We can't," I said. "That's what they call *dirty* money."

I explained about what my mother had said. About money and men.

"I don't get it," Ginny said.

I wasn't sure I completely did either, but I knew some-how that this money, all bright and shiny, was tied up with things I didn't want to think about.

"It's evil money. If we keep it, bad things will happen. All right? It's dirty money," I repeated. "We have to make a ceremony. We have to cleanse it. From that man."

"You think so?"

I could see by the way Ginny's skin went red that she had weird feelings about the man, too.

"I do. A ritual is required."

She nodded, solemn.

So I dug a hole and put the money in, tied with a white handkerchief and a sprig of cedar. I sprinkled church water over it, just in case. Then I filled up the hole and spat three times. And we left that money in her backyard, near the doghouse so Toby, her big mangy German shepherd, could guard it just like the wolf spirit my Aunt Shirley says stands guardian over me.

I think about that money, in the ground a whole year now, but Ginny never mentions it, and somehow I don't feel much like digging it up. I don't feel like doing much of anything this summer, except sitting up in the old apple tree out in the orchard. Sometimes, if I close my eyes and concentrate real hard, I can smell Aunt Shirley's clean sweet scent on the breeze. The smell of vanilla and wood-moss and rainfall.

# NICE GUY

The phone only rang once, so Steve figured his son Danny must have been waiting for his call.

"How you doing, sport?"

"Hey, Dad. I'm okay."

"How was school?"

"Okay."

"Got homework?"

"Yeah. You coming home soon?"

Steve rested his elbow on his thigh and pushed his fingers through his hair. He closed his eyes and imagined his son sitting on the leather stool, leaning on the dark blue tiles of the kitchen counter. He was probably picking at a scab. He pictured his son's bony knees. Steve wanted to protect him against all the sharp edges of the world but Danny was always banging into something or tripping over something.

"I don't know, sport. You know I love you, right? Right?"

"Yeah. Me, too."

"That's my guy. Listen, you think your mom will talk to me?"

"I'll ask her."

Even with Danny's hand over the phone, Steve heard Trish's muffled voice. He heard a cupboard slam, and in his mind's eye he imagined her holding her back ramrod straight as she marched out of the room, her long blond hair swinging against her sharp shoulder blades.

"Sorry, Dad, Mom says she can't talk right now. Man, she's really mad. You must'a done something this time." His ten-year-old voice was a whisper of awe.

"Okay, pal. No sweat. I'll talk to her later. And I'm gonna see you on Saturday. Listen, you don't worry about this. This isn't your problem, you know."

"I wish you'd come home, Dad."

"It's gonna be okay. Just a stupid grown-up thing. It's gonna be okay." When he hung up the phone, he reached for another bottle of beer. "Shit," he said.

Steve Bowman had left his wife two weeks ago, after she'd called him a waste of skin, *again*. All because he forgot to pick Danny up from hockey practice on Thursday when Trish worked night shift at the hospital. What was the big deal? The kid got home with some other mother, didn't he? Okay, he'd screwed up. He knew that. He'd said he was sorry, but Jesus, that woman could nag a man to death and a guy could only take so much. Blahda, blahda, blahda. The woman just never, ever, said uncle.

It wasn't like he'd ever hit her or even come close. He didn't cheat on her. But she said she couldn't rely on him, that she might as well go it alone if she couldn't depend on him. She'd ticked off his faults on her fingertips. A guy who was never there, who drank and hung out with his buddies too much, who forgot about his family, his responsibilities – in short, a guy like her father. A guy she didn't need.

"Christ, don't bring your father into this. Look, it won't happen again. Don't make such a big drama out of everything," he'd said.

"You don't even see me, do you?" she'd said.

"What the hell does that mean?" He couldn't help but laugh. Which he shouldn't have done.

"It means," she sneered the words out at him, mocking and nasty, "that you forgot? Like hell you did. You never even heard me. You care only about your own immediate gratification. You don't see us as individuals with needs and feelings of our own . . ."

"Oh shit, not the 'needs and feelings' speech." He put his hands over his ears, hoping she'd see the humour.

She put her hands on her hips and leaned into him. "You think it's funny, do you? You think it's funny I'm beginning to think I made a mistake here, a decade-long mistake?" Her eyes shone and her chin trembled. "How did I get stuck with this poor excuse for a man?"

He'd lost his temper then and said some things, like she was a fucking bull-dyke ball-breaker. He winced now, remembering that. He'd stomped out, leaving her yelling, "Don't you walk out on me, Steven Bowman, don't you do it!" as he headed for Harry's to knock back a few and cool down. When he'd gone back the light over the porch was off and she'd dead-bolted him out. She'd never done that before. Left him pounding on the door in the dark until Mr. MacAvey from next door threatened to call the cops. So now he was camped out on Harry's lumpy, spring-sprung sofa bed until he got his act together and found a place of his own. Or something.

Steve and Harry – the two musketeers, back together again. Living the way they had when they were college roommates. They ordered pizza or Chinese. They cracked open a bottle of Jack and some brew and stared at the boob tube. Harry's marriage hadn't lasted two years which, given Harry, Steve understood. But, after twelve years of, if not wedded bliss then at least good enough, Steve had thought he and Trish had made it. He couldn't figure out how it had blown apart.

In the early part of the evening, Steve and Harry talked about what bitches women were, but by midnight they were talking about how much they missed them.

Steve woke up every morning disgusted with himself and dragged his tail into the office, vowing to get it together and put an end to the self-pity. He sat all day staring at the stack of insurance claims the company paid him to process. Car crashes. Fires. Sewer back-ups. Lightning strikes. Frozen pipes. Disasters of all kinds. Not exactly the kind of stuff to improve a guy's outlook on life.

At first, there were nights when he drove past the house, just to catch a glimpse of Trish and Danny, just to see if the porch light was on. But the curtains were always closed and the front steps always dark, so after a while he stopped that.

Tonight he'd sworn off junk food. For an hour, he rattled and crashed around in the tiny kitchen alcove and surprised himself – made garlic bread and everything. Wasn't too bad, not as good as Trish's maybe, but not bad.

Harry thought Steve should call up some girl he knew named Crystal. "You'd like her, she's a cocktail waitress at this bar," he said, as he lugged himself up from the table to get a smoke. Harry sold cigarette vending machines and always seemed to have an endless supply of various brands. "She's got these great big tits and a little tiny waist and she's just what the doctor ordered, you know what I mean?"

"Naw. I don't think so."

"Back in the saddle, that's all I'm saying. You got to get back on the horse." Harry made a riding motion, legs bent, pelvis thrust forward, his hairy hands holding onto imaginary reins. "Giddy-up. Know what I mean?"

"Not my style. Besides, I'm still married, technically."

"Oh Christ, listen to this guy! You can't have it both ways, Stevie. Either you go back to that pussy-whipping wife of yours or you sing the praises of freedom! Freeeeedom!"

"Hey. I've said it before – don't talk about Trish like that. I get to. You don't." Steve looked at Harry over the top of his glasses, with an eyebrow arched, so he knew it was serious.

"Okay, point taken. No need to get hostile." He grinned and held his hands up as though to ward off a blow, which was a joke, considering Harry had at least a hundred pounds on Steve, and it wasn't all fat, either.

"Here, man, have a beer." Harry plunked a cold one on the table. He turned his chair around and rested his arms on the back.

"Yeah, all right. Forget it."

"All women are basically the same, is the way I see it. They want a man who's a real man and then when they get one, they want to change him. Turn him into something he wasn't meant to be. They will try and domesticate the wild thing which was what they once loved."

"You been reading too much of that *Iron John* crap," said Steve, peeling the label off his bottle. "Women want money and they want security and they want babies. Men just happen to fit into the equation as an afterthought." That didn't sound right – didn't sound like Trish. "Shit, I don't know. You don't think women want what we want?"

"And what the hell do we want?"

"Sex and food, peace and quiet," said Steve, "and love, I guess. Someone who understands you."

"I want love, true love, I want to tiptoe through the tulips and run through fields of daisies." Harry made a little bridge out of his fingers and rested his cheek against it, batting his eyes. "Oh yeah, and pussy, lots of pussy. And another Jack." He got up to get the bottle.

Steve thought about calling Harry on this, about reminding him of how he almost self-destructed when Cathy left him, but if it made him feel better to think of himself as a hard-ass, then Steve wasn't going to blow his cover.

"You are an irredeemable bastard, my friend. But it's why I love you and it's why there's no other couch I'd rather crash on. To Harry."

They toasted with whisky and slammed down the glasses.

Someone in the apartment next door put Marvin Gaye's "Sexual Healing" on the stereo.

"Let's get the hell out of here," Steve said.

Harry grinned. "Shank of the evening. Let's walk over to The Paddock."

The Paddock on a Wednesday night was not a pretty sight. At least on the weekends the crowds hid the stained orange carpet and gave the impression of a good time. Tonight there was only the washed-up, washed-out leftovers. The air smelled of smoke and stale beer. A TV hung over the bar with the sound turned off. On the screen two women fought, bent over, pulling hair and kicking. They reminded Steve of rams with their horns locked, if women could be rams. In one of the booths, four college-age guys in golf shirts and khaki pants and baseballs caps, with a pitcher of beer in front of them, laughed loudly. At one end of the bar sat a couple of grey old guys, unshaven and rumpled, drinking with silent determination. At the other end Ed the bartender leaned across the soda machine, talking to a woman with long black hair teased up into a kind of towering rat's nest, her fingers covered in heavy silver. She blew smoke rings. Ed stuck his finger through one and laughed. Steve and Harry headed for the bar stools. The bartender was a beefy guy with a black ponytail and a leather vest who limped as he walked over to them.

"What'll it be?" He chewed his words around a toothpick.

"Hey, Ed. Double Jack and a Bud," said Harry.

"Same," said Steve.

He brought them their drinks and went back down the bar to the woman. Steve realized she was staring at him – squinting through kohl-rimmed eyes. Steve broke away first.

"I think I'm going to Florida," said Harry.

"What? For a vacation?"

"I don't know. Not a vacation. Change of venue. Get me some sun. Get a house and a fishing boat in the Keys maybe."

"Fishing boat? What the hell do you know about fishing? And besides, you got a job."

"I hate my fucking job. I'm going to cash it in. You can have my apartment."

"I don't want your apartment."

"Why, what's wrong with it?"

"Nothing's wrong with it. I just don't want it."

"You think Trish's gonna let you back in. She won't." Harry slammed his fist down on the bar so suddenly that he startled the two old subterraneans at the end of the bar.

"Whatsa matter?" one of them said.

"Fucking women!" said Harry, then grabbed Steve by the shoulder. "You should come with me. We should get the hell out of this town. Go someplace where the weather isn't proof God's pissed off at us. I hate the fucking cold. We could do it, man. I'm telling you. We could really do it."

"I'm not going to Florida, Harry."

"Give me one good reason why not. Just one good reason."

"Danny. I'm not gonna leave my son, no matter what happens with me and Trish."

Harry's shoulders slumped. "Yeah. Danny. He's a great kid. He could come, too. I always wanted to teach a kid to fish."

"Trish would never let me take him."

"I guess not. But I'm going to Florida. Come spring. I'm gonna go."

"Sure you are, Harry."

"I am. But first, I'm going to take a piss." He stood up and had to take a little cross-legged two-step to get his balance. "Shit. I need another drink. Order us another. Jack and a beer."

Steve watched Harry head to the can and noticed the woman at the end of the bar still stared at him. She made him nervous. She said something to the bartender and he looked over at Steve, and then back at the woman and said something to her. They laughed, but the woman didn't sound like she thought it was so funny, whatever it was. She raised her tequila shot, licked salt off her other hand, and nodded at Steve. He smiled and wondered if she were a pro. He couldn't see her very well, with the light of the juke box behind her, but he didn't think she looked too good. He nodded but didn't smile.

"Hey, Ed, another couple Bud here, and a Jack for my friend."

"Sure thing. You wanted another shot, too?"

"Naw. I'm good."

"I'm drinking tequila," the woman said. "You wanna buy me a tequila?"

"Get the lady a drink."

There was something familiar about this woman. Steve wondered if he had seen her in the bar before.

"There you go, Elaine," said the bartender as he handed her the drink. Steve noticed it was a double. Oh, well. What the hell.

"Thanks, pal" she said and smiled again.

"You're welcome." *Elaine?* Why did this woman seem like someone he should know?

Harry came back, adjusting his fly.

"Hey, come here a minute," the woman called out to him as he passed.

"Me?"

"Who the hell else? Come here."

Harry looked at Steve, blinked once and then turned back to the woman, shrugged and walked over. Steve could not hear what she said, but Harry handed her a cigarette, even though she had a pack of her own on the bar. She bent her head toward the match Harry held and Steve could see her face better in the light. Her skin was bad. Pimples. Deep lines from her nose to her mouth and around her eyes. Her lipstick was nearly black and smeared. Damn, but she looked familiar. She said something to Harry and Harry looked over at Steve. The woman looked at Steve and winked. Then she turned back to Ed and ignored Harry. Harry stood for a moment, as if he didn't know he'd been dismissed and then came back to Steve.

"What was that all about?" said Steve.

"Chick says she knows you." Harry was looking at him strangely.

"Knows me? Who is she? She tell you her name?"

"Says her name is Elaine McKintey. Says you punched her in the stomach once."

"Oh, fuck!"

*Elaine McKintey.* It came back in a rush. He must have been about eleven. Elaine McKintey, the girl all the kids in school loved to tease, with her weird long greasy hair and black clothes and long sleeves even in the hot weather and bruises all over her legs. Always alone. Always leaning up against the fence, or huddled in a corner, twirling the ends of her hair. The girls cried out "Cooties, cooties!" and ran if they found themselves too near her. Elaine never said a word, just stared at her feet and scowled.

How had it happened that he and Elaine ended up in a stand-off? Why had she picked him out? Had he laughed at her or said something to her? He couldn't remember how it started, but he couldn't forget her eyes, flat as iron beneath her scraggly bangs as she said, "You think you're so smart, so tough, don't you?"

And he'd laughed.

"I could take you," she'd said through clenched teeth. "I could beat you up." Her body shook.

"You're a girl," he'd said, taken aback by her rage, shocked by the idea that a girl would even think about fighting. He'd never fought a girl. Why did she want to fight him?

"I dare you," she said. "I dare you to fight me. I want to fight you."

What could he do? All the kids looking on like that. He was *not* afraid of her.

"You're kidding," he'd said, which was stupid because Elaine was not someone who ever made a joke. "I'm not going to fight you. You're a girl." He hoped she'd back down.

"You're chickenshit," she said. "You're afraid. You ain't nothing." She spat. A practiced spit, the spit of a boy, not a girl, through her teeth. It landed on his running shoe.

He looked at the slimy mess on his nice clean kicks. "You want to fight, we'll fight."

So it had been arranged. After school, at the dead end of Baywood, where the street stopped and the forest began. She'd stood there, mittens stuffed into the pockets of her too-small navy pea jacket, bare grimy hands balled up into fists.

"Chickenshit," she kept taunting. "Go on, chickenshit, go for it. Take a shot."

The other kids had formed a circle, egging him on. "Go on, hit her. She's asking for it. Teach her a lesson. Go on!"

"Chickenshit, chickenshit, chickenshit . . ." Over and over she kept singing it at him and sneering, her lips curled over yellow teeth.

He wanted her to move first, to go for him, so he could feel like he was defending himself at least. He didn't want to hit her, didn't want to hit a girl. But with every taunt he hated her more for putting him in this position. It was her fault. He needed to put an end to it.

"Whatsa matter, little boy, little mama's boy? Whatsa matter, little chickenshit?"

It was the look on her face that did it. The look that said she was better than he was, that she was winning. He just had to make her stop looking like that.

He punched her in the stomach.

He'd never knocked the wind out of anyone before and he didn't know what had happened. Elaine's hands came up in a reflex, her fingers spread wide. She bent over a little, but did not double up. Her face turned red. She opened her mouth once or twice, but kept a sort of grin on her face, like this was just what she wanted.

Nobody said anything. His breathing was ragged and shallow. Sweat made his clothes itch, but he didn't put his hands down to scratch. He was sure she'd come at him as soon as she got some air in her lungs.

She took a halting breath, but never took her eyes from his face.

"Is that it? Is that the best you can do? Hell," she said in a whisper that gave not a single inch, "my mother can hit harder than that."

There was something in the way she said it. Something in her eyes that didn't seem to be seeing him at all anymore, that made him understand. What she said was true. Elaine McIntey's mother hit harder than any boy. He knew then that she had to hit him back. She had to. That would make it all right and maybe they could walk away with no harm done. If she would just hit him back, really wallop him. And how much could it hurt with her wrists like pipe-cleaners?

"So, you're such a big mouth – go ahead and take your best shot," he said. Elaine smiled at him but didn't move. "Go on, this is your big chance, I'm giving you a chance here."

"I don't need to hit you," she said, and he could see she was mad as hell, but she wouldn't move. She just stood there in the slushy snow, her down-at-the-heel loafers soaking wet and her socks hanging down over bluish, bony ankles. "Tough is taking it," she said. "That's what heart is, that's what Marciano had. Heart." And with that she turned and walked away, her back stiff and straight and her legs a little wobbly, but she didn't go down.

*Elaine McKintey. Jesus!*

"What is she, some old girlfriend?" said Harry.

"No. Not exactly." He tried not to look up at the end of the bar. "We went to school together."

"She looks older than you. She looks a mess. Cracked out. When did you see her last?"

"Must be twenty years. She left school at sixteen, disappeared. I thought she went out West someplace."

Elaine was looking at him. She dipped her finger in her drink and then stuck it in her mouth, sucking on it.

"Shit, you think she's a hooker?" Steve said.

"No doubt. You gonna avail yourself though, you better take this."Harry reached in his pocket, fumbled, and dropped something on the floor. He bent over to pick it up. "Here," he said, and held out a condom.

"Put that away, you asshole." Steve couldn't just sit here. He had to go over. It was the least he could do. "I'm going over."

"Sure you don't want this?" said Harry, holding out the small plastic square. Steve ignored him.

She wore a black long sleeved T-shirt, with a tear near the armhole. Black stretchy pants and a wide belt. She was so skinny her bones showed through the fabric. There were bruises on the back of her hand. Her eyes sat deep in shadowed hollows.

"Hey, Elaine."

"Steve Bowman." She blew smoke in his face. He ignored it and sat down on the stool next to her.

"It's been a long time. Nice to see you again."

"Yeah. Okay," she said. "Nice to see me."

"I heard you were out in Vancouver."

"Nope. Always been here."

"Ah. So, how are you?"

"How do I fucking look?" She turned to face him and the light from the juke box shone full on her. Her skin was slack and he saw that what he had thought were pimples were actually small lesions.

"You look good."

"You're a liar. I know how I look. I'm sick."

"Shit. I'm really sorry."

"Occupational hazard." She shrugged. Her shoulder bones threatened to rip through the thin fabric of her T-shirt.

"I'm sorry."

"Why?"

"Why what?" He looked to Ed for help, but the bartender moved down the bar to get the two rummies at the end another round.

"You married?" she said. "You look married."

"Yeah. Trish Elliot. You remember Trish Elliot."

"Nope."

"Sure you do, you remember Trish."

"I don't remember much from those days. I make an exception for you."

"Why for me?" Might as well get it over with. He could say he was sorry.

"Because you didn't ignore me. You were a nice guy. Everybody else treated me like I was either invisible or diseased." She stubbed out her cigarette. "Ironic, huh? I mean considering the circumstances now. Fucking ironic. Timing is everything. Yeah, you were a nice guy and I hated you."

"You hated me?"

"Not just you, but all of you – floating around in your little superior worlds. Maybe you most of all. I couldn't wait to get away from you all. From everything. Joke. What the hell did I know? Nobody does anything. Nothing changes. What the hell did I know?" She turned away from him, back to her drink. "Ed. Ed! Jesus, Ed! Get me another drink. My old friend here's paying."

"Sure, no problem. Listen, I could let you have some money if you're short, you know."

"Go home to your wife, Stevie."

"It's no problem." He pulled out a couple of twenties and left them on the bar. She pushed them back at him.

"No, I'm stubborn. I got that left," she said. "Now, go away."

"Yeah. Okay. I should go. You take care of yourself, Elaine."

Ed brought the bottle of tequila and a plate of limes.

"Pour," she said to Ed, and ignored Steve. He walked back to Harry.

"That's it. It's finished. I'm going back," said Steve, heading for the door.

"What did she say?" Harry followed him.

"She said I was a nice guy."

"Ouch. Strike out."

"I'm going home," said Steve.

"Yeah, fine," said Harry.

"No, I don't mean your home. I mean my home. I'm going to get in a cab and I'm going to go home and I'm going to sit outside all night if I have to and I'll sit there all day tomorrow if I have to."

"I don't know, man. I think we should go to Florida." Harry slapped him on the back and then hung on as the cold air hit him. "Whoa, I'm dizzy."

Steve took Harry home. He packed up his suitcase and called a cab. All the way across town he thought about how he would beg Trish's forgiveness and listen to everything she had to say. He was going to agree with her because she was, after all, probably right, and even if she wasn't he did not really care. Tonight he was going to sleep in his own bed, with his wife – his tough, stubborn, beautiful wife – and he was going to spend the rest of his life being a nice guy.

When the cab pulled up, he saw the dark porch. And as the cab pulled off again he stood there and stared at it. It nearly broke his heart, those shadows did. It didn't matter though. No amount of darkness was going to stop him. He picked up his suitcase and walked up to the door and rang the bell. He couldn't breathe. For a long time nothing happened. And then the light switched on and when it did small cracks ran through his chest, like a windshield hit by a stone. Fractures spread everywhere through him and it hurt, almost more than he could stand. But he stood it. He had to. He had to be tough for his love's sake.

# SURPRISE

It is the sort of diner where nothing much happens, where people know each other, where Benny, the cook, uses canned, industrial filling in the pies, and the coffee is bitter, if hot. Customers come in waves and sit in the same seats every time. Donna, the waitress, calls everyone "hon," which Benny doesn't like especially, but that's information he keeps to himself. The menu hasn't changed since 1984, and some of the old guys mumble that it was probably the last time the grease trap was cleaned, too. Some things don't change much. Some people like it that way. Others? Well.

Donna watches the new guy. He sat in the same seat every day for the past eight days. Pretends he's reading the paper, or picking ponies, but she's not buying it. Donna figures this guy's been in prison. She can tell. Around here, you get to know the signs. First thing, it's the grey, paper-pale complexion. Fish skin, she calls it. Then it's the clothes. Clean maybe but, in this case, at least twenty years out of style. And the guys who've been inside for a while, they don't say a whole lot. There are two kinds of ex-cons: the kind who can't take the quiet, who have to keep tapping and banging on things all the time, and the kind who can't get enough of it. This guy's the second kind, the kind that gives Donna the spooks. It makes her feel better knowing Big Benny's in the back, even if he doesn't come out much after the lunch rush. The guy motions to her. Wants another coffee.

The man sits in the window alcove of the slim and grimy restaurant. He orders a coffee, then another and finally a third. Now and then, he glances at the clock that hangs moon-pale over the microwave on the back wall. He looks out the smudgy window. The leaves on the trees are the colour of old limes and the trunks are dark as treacle. He doesn't like autumn weather. It makes him feel brittle inside, as if he could snap at any moment.

He knows the waitress – Donna, if the name tag is right – watches him and he knows she wishes he weren't so quiet, because the first two days he came in she tried to make small talk, pestered him with her "How you doing, hon's?" and her "You been away for a while, huh's." On the third day, he'd brought a newspaper with him and hid behind that whenever she approached. On the fourth day, he brought a newspaper *and* a racing form. She took the hint, finally. Now he sits, watching the street, seemingly with no purpose. His fleshy, liver-spotted hands wrap and unwrap around the thick porcelain of his cup. He never takes off his coat. Now and then his lips move, forming soundless words. He sips his coffee. He's waiting, but he's used to that. It's no hardship to wait, and he has nowhere to go, nothing else to do. He stays until the light fades. He doesn't like to be out of his room after dark. The world is a changed place and he's not used to the vast bland sky above him, nor to the groups of rough boys and thickly made-up girls in baggy pants, backward hats and heavy gold jewellery who bluster through the evening streets like packs of hungry hounds, snarling "Where you at?" into tiny wireless phones. At night, he feels like a rat caught outside his hole.

During the day, it's all right. In fact, during the day he can't stay in his room. During the day, the dull light from the airshaft outside his window crawls into every corner of the room and pushes up against the walls. He can't breathe in there. So he comes here, to this lunch counter restaurant. He rehearses words in his head. That's what he does, hour after hour. It was lucky, finding a place right across the street. Like it was supposed to be this way. He'll make his move when the words are right. But not until then. Because the words have to be impeccable, perfect.

Once the evening begins to set in, he leaves the lunch counter and finds his way back to his room in the boarding house. He looks in shop windows on his walk, amazed, especially at the computer equipment and video games. It's one thing, seeing this stuff on TV in the prison day room, and another to see it as a thing possible to use oneself. It's like living in the middle of a *Star Trek* episode. He doesn't like it. It makes too many sounds, moves too fast, ends too quickly. Like everything these days. When he first got out, government cheque in hand, too old now for anyone to demand of him a decent day's work, he'd bought a television set. Just a small one, but after a week he got rid of it. Gave it to Eddie

Fry, the young turk in the next room, who was still a long way off from where *he* was. Eddie still had a chance at figuring out a legal way to live in this place, this time.

Even in jail, he'd never watched television much. Maybe sometimes a ball game. But the room was always too noisy, too crowded, too smoky, too full of the thick funk of violent possibilities. He had preferred the forgotten quiet of the small, windowless prison library, or, failing that, the bed-sized space of his own territory.

Popular culture passed him by while he read. Thomas Mann. Pearl S. Buck. Fitzgerald. Hemingway. C.S. Lewis. Carl Jung. Plato. Yes, even him, the old fascist.

When he was not reading he wrote. At first, he wrote page after page of profanity, venom, and furious ranting. Directed to himself, of course, for it had always been himself he'd hated. He was never one of those guys who said it was all a mistake, he didn't remember, or the gun had just gone off, or the knife was just there, suddenly, in his hand.

When even self-loathing wore thin, he wrote stony, hollow words of despair. Then, for several piercing, bloody years, he wrote prayers. Then he wrote letters to her, the only person he knew to write, but they all came back unopened, the stamp of one government services office or another on them. Then they came back because she was gone, with no forwarding address. He wrote to her anyway.

It kept him sane. Even when the notebooks were stolen, were used to wipe the shit from his cellmates' asses, used to light somebody's cigarette, used as fodder for the taunting, brutal day-to-day indignities any normal person would consider too cruel, too barbaric to survive – even then, he clung to the words. By the time he was able to leave, he thought he had the gist of it, of what he had to say, of what would save him.

It hadn't been hard to find her, once he got out. A telephone book. That's all it had taken. And he'd thought the fact she didn't have an unlisted number was a good sign. Maybe she was leaving out a breadcrumb for him to find. It gave him hope.

He'd sat in the window and waited, unsure at first if he'd even recognize her. It had been that long. A lifetime. What if she passed by and he didn't know her? Would that be possible? Every morning he sat in bed and studied the picture he had of her, taken when she was only six, in grade one.

He'd sat at the same table, jangled and stiff with longing, for two days. Then he'd seen her.

The coat caught his attention. The red coat. Even as a little girl, she'd always loved red coats. And red rubber boots for jumping in puddles. Here she was, walking down the street, wearing a red woollen coat, with a black purse slung over her shoulder, carrying a plastic bag of groceries and holding the hand of a little boy.

The coffee cup was halfway to his mouth when he recognized her. Donna had just poured it for him and he spilled some on his thigh and burned himself, but he didn't move. He was afraid a fast movement would catch her eye, afraid she'd turn and see him, afraid she'd run. He stopped breathing. Blood bloated his face as his heart nearly burst. It took every ounce of willpower not to rush out into the street.

Then, she pulled open the heavy door of the building and disappeared.

He got up from the table and went into the bathroom. He went into the stall and sat down on the toilet. He pulled a long strip of toilet paper from the roll and buried his face in it. He stayed like this for some minutes until he heard someone clear his throat and he saw Benny's big feet under the stall door. Benny whistled tunelessly and made a loud point of washing his hands. The man stood up, flushed the toilet and walked out, turning his face away from Benny as he went to the sink and splashed cold water on his burning eyes.

He left his space in the window alcove early that day, too buffeted by emotion to sit still. He went to the park. He sat on a bench under an elm tree and watched the squirrels rush about in frenzied preparation for the oncoming winter. The boy had surprised him. But of course, it made sense. She was a woman now. She wasn't a little girl anymore. The idea that there might also be a man, a husband or boyfriend, set him back a bit. Somehow he hadn't figured anyone else into the scene. He'd always thought it would be just him and her. He didn't know how to approach her if she were with a man. Maybe the man would hit him. Well, that would be all right. He'd been hit before. The boy looked about eight, and had his grandmother's dark hair and blue eyes.

The man returned to the same window seat the next day, and the next and the next and the one after that, watching, waiting to see it there was a husband. But it seemed she was alone. This made him feel more confident, but it also made him sad to think she was alone in the world, that maybe she hadn't been any more successful in her relationships than he'd been. Well, that wouldn't be true though, would it? No, even divorced, abandoned, betrayed, she'd be more successful than him. But perhaps, if she was finding it difficult to be alone, and raising a child, perhaps there'd be a place for him, someone to lend a hand. He had so much to make up for.

On the tenth day of his vigil, he believes the time has come. He has perfected his speech, he has honed his words to their clear, true purpose, so that only the essential truth of the thing will shine through, unmarred, unblemished by even the faintest taint of impurity. His long pilgrimage is almost over. He settles himself. He takes a deep breath and stands. He walks out the door, not bothering to close it behind him.

Donna frowns as a dust devil of street trash swirls in – a paper coffee cup. She walks to the door, muttering about how thoughtless people are, meaning to pick it up and toss it in the garbage bin. She sees the new guy in the street, realizes he hasn't paid for his coffee and is about to yell at him, then stops. He's focused on something and her eyes follow his. Across the street a youngish woman in a bright red coat and a child are talking with another woman, an old, layered-up, baggy sort of woman. The youngish woman holds the little boy's hand. The little boy has a Power Ranger doll, a blue one, sticking out of the top of his duffel coat pocket. The woman has soft blond hair and freckles across the bridge of her bent little nose.

The man does not hurry but steps cautiously. He approaches her smoothly; the way a cowboy might approach a horse, with a lead in one hand, looped behind his back where the horse can't see it.

Donna steps out onto the street. There's a wind up, and a sprinkle of rain.

"Surprise!" the man says, in a high-pitched voice.

The expression on the woman's face is such that Donna doesn't really think it's such a surprise after all.

"Benny," Donna calls to the cook. "Benny, come look at this!"

The young woman in the red coat says something to the old woman, and the old woman scuttles away, calling out something that might be "help" but then again might not be.

Benny lumbers out from the kitchen, a spatula in his hand, and stands behind Donna.

The woman pushes the little boy behind her.

"Go away," she says to the man. "Go away."

"I didn't mean to say that – surprise, I mean. Stupid. Sorry. I just want to talk."

"No," says the woman. "Leave us alone!"

"Five minutes. Please. I need to tell you . . ."

"No," she says again, and looks up the street and down the street and then across the street to Donna and Benny.

"Please, listen . . . You're the only family I have, now."

"Whose fucking fault is that?! Whose? Are you insane?" says the woman, her eyes bright, and her mouth hard. She runs up the building steps, dragging the boy after her. She fumbles with her keys, and then with the lock on the door.

"I just want to explain," says the man. He stays on the bottom step, but his hands reach out towards the woman. "I need to tell you . . ."

The woman turns, pulls back her head and spits at the man, the slick, slimy wad landing right in the middle of his face. He doesn't wipe if off.

"I don't want to hear it! How could you ever fucking explain? If you ever come near us again, I'll kill you, do you hear me! You son of a bitch!" She grabs the little boy roughly. She scrambles into the building, pushes the heavy glass and steel door shut, checks to make sure the lock has caught, and disappears.

"Poor old fart," says Benny.

"You think so?" says Donna.


The man ascends the steps, stands heavily in front of the door and puts his palm up on it, as though checking for some residual warmth. He leans his forehead against it. Softly, he bangs his head. His fragile words melt on the fire of his tongue, dissolve like snowflakes. He pushes himself straight, pulls a tissue out of his pocket, and wipes away the spit. He puts the tissue back in his pocket. He turns around and sees Donna and the cook watching him, sees the old

woman huddled in a doorway, sees some neighbours looking, sees some people on the sidewalk staring. He comes
down the stairs, holding onto the banister for support and
begins to shuffle down the street, with small, slow, old man
steps.

"Hey, buddy," Donna calls. "You didn't pay for your coffee."

The man stops and puts his hands up to his face, making
swiping motions. Then he turns, rummaging in his pants
pockets, walking toward Donna. She makes a motion, as
though she's going to step behind Benny, but then she
stands her ground.

"Here," the man says, and hands her a ten-dollar bill.

"Don't you have anything smaller? I'll have to go in and
get you change."

"No. Doesn't matter." He doesn't move away, but stands
there, looking at Donna and Benny, his chin trembling.

"I wasn't going to hurt her," he says. "I never hurt her. I
wouldn't do that."

"Sure," says Benny. "Sure."

"I just wanted to talk. I had all these words ready. The
right words, and then these other words came out. Stupid
words. How could that happen?"

"Don't think you better come around here no more, mister," says Benny.

The man deflates, like he's been holding himself up,
holding his breath. "No," he says. "No, I guess not." He
walks away, his throat stuffed with sound, not bothering to
close his coat against the leaf-wet wind.

Across the street, at a curtainless window on the second storey, the youngish woman stares after the old man, her hand held up, fingers covering her mouth.

# LAST CUP OF TEA
# WITH BEN

The tree tosses twigs against the window. Rain in sheets so thick I can't see out. I have the perfect fire going and am snuggled on the couch, halfway through *A Winter's Tale*.

The phone rings. It's Danielle, Ben's wife.

"I don't know what to do with him," she says. "He wants to be around you. I need a couple of hours to myself. Is it okay?"

I tell her it's okay. "We'll have one of our tea parties." Ben and I often spent an afternoon over tea, solving the problems of the universe, arguing about politics, literature, and music. We hadn't done it in a while though, not since the accident.

"If it gets too bad, call me," says Danielle.

"Is he worse?"

Her breathing over the line is uneven. "He had some kind of experience. I don't know." There are tears in her voice, and the sound of her swallowing them.

"He'll be fine here for a while," I say. "Take some time for yourself."

Fifteen minutes later the doorbell rings.

Ben stands dripping on the porch. He wears a yellow ski jacket, too small even on his skinny frame, and an ear-warmer headband. His glasses are fogged and slip down his nose.

"Come on in." I kiss him on the cheek.

He shuffles into the hallway, water streaming from his pant cuffs. He takes tiny steps, not lifting his feet off the ground. He's only forty-two but he moves like an old man in bedroom slippers.

The problems started with the car accident in Rome last fall and he'd been getting worse ever since. Although the accident hadn't been that bad, a twisted neck, a few bruises, it triggered some sort of tear in the centre of who he was.

We go to the kitchen and I make tea. He sits watching me and talks in stops and starts, like a car with a clutch that won't catch.

"I still feel the pain in my neck, all the time, can't sleep, can't move without this . . . tingling all the way down my arm. The doctor says I should be taking Valium . . . to slow, myself down but I don't want to take that. I could freak out. You know, and that would be . . . I can't take medication. I never could take, anything that changes me. Does that make sense?"

"You took some the other night when Phil and I were with you and it helped, didn't it?" I put a cup of strong tea in front of him and sit down at the table.

"That was different. You were there. In case, anything happened. But, all that's . . . changed now, I think." He leans forward. His fingers play an invisible piano on his knees. "I've seen God," he whispers, closing the distance between us. His breath is on my face. It smells of milk.

"Drink your tea," I say.

The look on his face frightens me. Intent. Wolfish. A zealot's expression. Ben has always laughed at what he called "The God Squad," and I used to find his sarcasm irritating.

"I want to . . . tell you about it, you'll . . . understand."

"Okay," I say, although I'm not sure that it is.

"I was walking, in the . . . woods, right? Then it happened."

He sits back in his chair, face tilted upward, and he focuses on a spot above my head.

"All the, trees began to glow, the rocks. And the ferns and . . . things. Everything. A sparrow. Squirrel. God was in everything. I felt His pain."

Tears run unchecked down his cheeks and drip from his chin, leaving dark splotches on his already stained sweatshirt. I want to hand him a tissue, tell him to stop. I want him to be the old Ben, irreverent, sarcastic, sharp as a shark's tooth.

"God, weeps for us," he says. "You can't begin. To comprehend. His anguish because. Of us." He speaks in three-quarter time.

He makes no effort to wipe his face or his plugged nose. It makes me slightly ill. I feel as though I'm being made to look at something I have no right to see, something that should be private. I want to turn away.

"I felt, energy all, around, the whole world alive." He looks at me with sparkling eyes.

There's so little left of Ben now. The man who studied Japanese and palaeolithic art in his spare time. The financial whiz kid who invested and re-invested and retired at thirty-eight, a self-made multi-millionaire.

I reach for a box of tissue.

"Blow your nose, Ben." He does what he's told.

"Do you, think we can relieve God's suffering?" he says. A feral, eager cunning lights his face, and the query, I suspect, conceals a plan. He is a wraith-image of what he once was: a cocky, confident man who often asked a question not to know your answer but to lead you to his own. He used to love verbal jousts. Now the sincerity of his question is hallucinogenic, fracturing.

"I don't know." I sit back in my chair. Every inch counts. "But maybe He can relieve ours."

"It's the same thing," says Ben. His hands grip the teacup. He strains toward me.

"You had a very powerful experience." I don't know what he wants. My hands are clasped so tightly that my wedding ring digs into my finger.

"I need to confess," he says.

This is when the penny drops. Crafty, very crafty, I think.

He gets up, moving back and forth between the door and the table. My kitchen feels too small. I take deep breaths.

"Will you hear my sins?"

I've known Ben and his wife Danielle for long enough to know I do not want to hear this confession. His infidelities are, if not common knowledge, no tightly guarded secret either. I don't think, close as I am to his wife, that I should know these things.

"I don't want to hear this, Ben."

"But, it should, be you. We're connected, don't you think?"

I know what he's talking about. Ben and I didn't meet until three years ago, but found we had a lot in common. Twisted roots, twisted family backgrounds. Childhoods where sometimes your mother gets crazy sick and goes away for a while and comes home like somebody you don't know – quiet, with her hair all lank and her eyes all flat.

For years, I'd fallen to the bottom of a Stoli bottle, trying to block it out, but the undertow of the booze nearly drowned me and I had to surface, ring myself dry and find a way to live. I built a safe place where the ghosts couldn't hurt me. I thought Ben had found a way to handle his ghosts too. He's so smart. And although he'd always been eccentric, he'd been okay, until the accident.

Who would have thought a busted axle and a twisted steering wheel would shake out so much anguish?

"I think you're worn down, Ben, from the pain in your back. You need to take it easy."

"I wrote a poem. Want, to hear it?" He stands at the end of the table, stiff and straight, like a little boy in front of the class. His hands are fists in front of him, and look like little rodent paws. "Okay, I'm going to tell my poem."

I don't know how to make him stop. He should stop.

"Bad man, walking down the street, Old tin can kicked at his feet, I'm a tin can from the Tin Can Man." He stops. "That's all I have so far."

"It's nice," I say. "You should keep working on it."

He sits down again. I want to steer him back to the world that waits for him. I want to see us both through these treacherous waters.

"You used to play with Carly every day, Ben. Do you still play with your daughter?"

"Danielle needs to spend more time. With me," he says, which is an answer to my question, in a way. "She's my wife. She, says I get on her nerves now, but why can't she take care, of me?" He crosses his arms against his chest, and he pouts. "You take care of Phil when he's sick. You, bring him soup."

We're not going to go down that road. I've felt Ben push this way before, a little wedge in the door, trying to make room for three, where only two will do. My flesh crawls at this mother-skin he's trying to fit me into.

"It'll get better. Just take it slow and easy. Have some more tea." I pour his old tea, untouched and cold, into the sink, and pour him fresh.

"I'll get better when I cleanse myself. Become the man God wants me to become. I need to tell you, the things I've done. For God's sake."

"I'm not comfortable with this."

"Why can't you, be the one?"

"It's just not a good idea, Ben."

He is stubborn now and hollow with need. My face hardens. I feel it turn into the same old perfect passive plane, giving nothing away. Taking nothing in. We go round and round some more, until I feel like I'm nine years old again, in another kitchen, with someone else who didn't know where I ended and where she began. There's a terrible familiar intimacy in the air. I know he wants me to be his confessor for this reason. He wants to become my past and wants me to become his, because that's the real crazy glue.

This is why my mother did what she did when she knew I would be the one to find her: because to be chosen to know the sin is to be connected forever. The demoniac's complicity.

"I need to get back to work, Ben. Do you want me to call Danielle to drive over and pick you up? The weather's worse."

"Okay," he says. "I don't want, to be too much for, you. I'm afraid you won't want to see me anymore. I don't, want to wear you out." He pats the table in quick little movements with the palms of his hands.

"You're not," I say. "You can come back and we'll come to see you."

I call Danielle and she arrives with Carly, who doesn't run and jump into my arms like she used to. Maybe she's too grown up for that now. Seven, as I remember, can be a hard age.

When Ben has his coat on, he says, "I have to, go to the bathroom," and goes into the toilet by the front door. We hear him talking to us, but must move closer to make out the words. Danielle and Carly stand by the door casually, but I don't want to. I'm suffocating. He calls my name. I move closer and hear him talking, and other noises, too. Danielle and I don't look at each other.

"Do you want me to use, the air freshener, or just open the, window?" he finally says.

"Open a window," I say. We hear him flush.

He opens the door and holds out his arms for me to hug him. His smell follows. I have to stop from pushing him away.

We say good-bye and when he's gone I go into the living room, open the window and stick my head out. I let the rain hit my face until I'm cold and filled with the scent of pine needles and wet earth and the tang of winter coming on the wind.

Danielle calls two days later. They're going back to New York, where Ben's cousin is a psychiatrist. They're looking into beds and treatment.

"What if he doesn't get better?" she says.

"He'll get better," I say, because I've learned the necessity of being hopeful.

"Christ," she says, in the voice of a widow at a wake. "I miss the old Ben."

I bow my head. "Me, too," I say.

# GESTURES

"Oh God, Brian, not another one of those business things," Candace said. It was after 11 p.m., and she was tired. Most of their dinners were late, if they managed to eat together at all. And yes, she knew that Parisians often ate late in the evening, but she didn't think they ate *this* late. "Do I have to go?"

"Yes. You have to go." He rattled the demitasse. "Jesus, you're always complaining I'm never around and then when I include you, you start whining."

"It's just that hours spent making small talk with strangers isn't my idea of a great evening."

"It's business. You don't have to like it. You just have to do it – gracefully. You knew to expect this when we came to Paris. If we'd been transferred to Cleveland, I doubt you'd have the burden. But no, Candace, you live in Paris. There's a price to pay."

As there is for everything, she thought. "Couldn't we go out for dinner alone sometime?"

"We're eating alone now, aren't we?"

"A hurried meal in the middle of the night isn't what I mean. I mean, you know, Paris. Most romantic city in the world, and all that."

"You should spend more time counting your blessings and less complaining. You'd be happier," he said and walked out of the room, leaving her to fume at the uncleared table.

Candace stuck her index finger in her mouth and pursed her lips around it. Her mother had taught her this trick to make sure she didn't get lipstick on her teeth. She pulled her finger out, wiped off the excess *Berrystain Red,* and bared her teeth in the mirror just to make sure. She smiled. For a woman closer to 40 than 30, she looked pretty damned good.

As she dabbed perfume on the backs of her knees and the inside of her wrists, she reviewed the information Brian had given her about the clients: Albert and Sharon MacDonald. Albert is Vice-President of Preston Steel. Grant Carter, General Director of Amalgam Inc., and his wife Linda. Their first time in Paris. Very Important Clients.

Another evening of playing the corporate wife – dress pretty and be the gracious hostess. Part of the contract. Fair enough. She would fulfill her agreement and try not to think of her marriage as part of this contract. She would show the Very Important Clients the real Paris. Not the touristy Paris, with its Eiffel Tower lineups and flashbulb-garish Latin Quarter, but the elegant cloistered Paris that nestled in the shadows of the side streets. She would impress them with how at home she was in Paris. After four years of living here her French was good enough. Most importantly though, she'd finally broken the fashion code. Tonight's thin black skirt, crisp white shirt, high heels, and scarf were just right. Her softly curled blond hair was chic. Brian would be pleased with her, which would make the evening easier. Detecting a stray smear of lipstick, she stuck her finger in her mouth again.

"Do you have any idea how sexy it is when you do that?" Brian stood behind her, watching her in the mirror.

"Yes," she grinned, "I do." Brian liked sexy. It was a softening agent Candace had learned to use.

He kissed her cheek and told her she looked beautiful. She straightened his tie. Hugged him, breathing in his aftershave. A woman took the good moments when she could.

"I love you," she said. And she did. Big, solid, successful, brown-eyed Brian. The man who'd taken her from her little life in Peterborough to the adventure of France. The man who'd promised her a life free from financial worry and who had been as good as his word. The envy of her friends. The apple of even her mother's critical eye. The perfect man.

"You could almost pass for a Parisian," he said.


At the hotel, the three couples sat on leather chairs in the pleasant, ferny bar and drank *kir*. The women becoming acquainted in their way, by sharing slight intimacies, the men in theirs, by talking business.

"So tell me," said Candace, "what do you want to do while you're here? Museums? Shopping? Churches?"

"I haven't really decided," said Sharon. "I went out for a bit today, to see the shops, but I can't say I was very impressed. Everything's so expensive." Sharon held her hard brown purse on her lap. Now and then she reached up to pat the front of her blue flowered dress, as though reassuring herself the dolphin brooch was still in place. "All the clothes look like they're for kids."

"What's the name of the department store everyone talks about?" said Linda. Linda had long acrylic nails and a fluff of frazzled red hair. She wore a black suit with yellow piping along the edges and gold buttons on the pockets.

"I think you mean Gallerie Lafayette," said Candace. "But you might find the smaller shops more fun."

"I'm not looking for anything kooky," said Sharon.

"At least they speak English in the big stores," said Linda.

Candace thought it might be safer to move on to museums and tried to interest the ladies in the smaller museums, like the Rodin, or the Picasso. But Sharon and Linda preferred the Louvre, which the two agreed had all the important works.

"Our education in art's limited to what goes over the sofa, I'm afraid," Grant joined in, with a gummy smile plastered across his wide freckled face.

Brian said, "We've made a reservation at *L'affriole*, which is very good. The new cuisine."

"Just good old normal food for us," said Albert. "Nothing fancy."

"We can go anywhere you like," said Brian. "We can eat Italian or Chinese, even. Or we can just eat here at the hotel if you'd prefer." Candace watched the smile tighten slightly around the edges of Brian's mouth.

"No, I'm sure we'll be fine," said Sharon, "as long as it's not anything weird."

"We'll make sure you don't get *ris-de-veau*," said Candace, trying to lighten the mood. "You know, calves' thyroid and pancreas."

"Calves what?!?" said Sharon.

Brian pursed his lips, glared at her and gave a tiny shake of his head.

"No, I'm kidding. Don't worry."

"It'll be fine, dear," said Albert. He patted his wife's plump arm.

They arrived at the restaurant and Madame Cuvet seated them at a good table at the end of the lovely Bell Époque room. Gilt mirrors lined the walls and lamps hung like lettuce-pale tulips from the bronze ceiling.

Menus arrived. The long chaotic chore of translating began, with everyone speaking at once. Sharon piped up every so often, saying, "Are you *sure* they wouldn't have an English menu?" After ten minutes, Madame came to take their order, but they still needed more time. Madame arched her eyebrow and smiled encouragingly to Candace, seated at the far end of the table, next to Grant. She'd talked him round to the *Rasscasse au basilic*. She despaired of finding a dish on the menu that pleased Albert.

"Just a good piece of meat for me, sweetheart. Don't worry about any extras."

They settled on *Le bifteck aphrodisiaque*, although Albert looked skeptical.

Brian tried to herd Sharon in the direction of a choice. He began to waggle his fork up and down like a wobbly little boat between his index fingers. A sure sign of distress. Candace's stomach fluttered. She had to get the evening back on course. She leaned around Grant.

"Sharon, what do you think? Anything tempt you?"

"Brian thinks I should have the chicken with garlic but forty cloves sounds like too much to me. Can that be right?"

Madame Cuvet hovered, as severe in her chic black suit as Sister Mary Michael from Candace's grade-four class.

"You'll love it, trust me," said Candace, and Sharon reluctantly agreed. Brian stopped waggling the cutlery. He turned, with much relief, and gave Madame their order.

They settled back with a glass of champagne. Candace did her best to look fascinated every time someone used the word "smelting."

A small, sharp cry silenced the table. It was Sharon.

"Honey, are you all right?" said Albert.

Sharon held her napkin up to the side of her face and pointed to the man sitting on the banquette next to her.

"He's smoking!" she said, as though she had caught him with his hands down his pants.

"Oh dear," said Albert. "You'd better change seats with me."

Sharon flapped her napkin. "I don't want to be rude, but really."

"C'mon then, honey. Change seats with me."

The tables were very close together and had to be pulled into the aisle so Sharon could get out. Brian, Linda and

Albert all stood. Sharon squeezed past. The offending smoker grabbed his carafe of water in order not to have it swept to the floor with a mighty shake of Sharon's outraged rump.

Sharon stood and looked around the restaurant. "They are *all* smoking," she said, in what she apparently intended to be a whisper. Candace blushed and snapped her fingers down on her palms as though playing an invisible pair of castanets, a nervous habit she'd had since childhood.

"I'm sure you'll be fine down at the end if you don't like smoke," said Brian. He pulled out the chair for her, encouraging her to sit down.

"I'm very sorry. I have allergies. I can't tell you how sorry I am. I was looking forward to this, really I was."

"Sorry folks," said Albert, with a quick wave. "Happens all the time. She's very sensitive to smoke. Guess we should have thought of that."

"Are they going?" said Linda after a moment.

"Apparently," said Brian, who looked as though someone had poured cold water on him. He looked pointedly at Candace and said, "Wish I'd known about that before we decided to come here."

"Well, she should have said something before," said Linda. "Can't be expected to read her mind, now can you?"

And they could all see the sense in that, although Candace knew Brian likely held her responsible. "Would anyone like another glass of champagne?" she said, not meeting Brian's eyes. "Don't you think we should have another glass?"

As the evening ended and Grant and Linda were safely deposited at their hotel, Candace and Brian walked to the Metro.

"Grant and Linda aren't so bad. A bit narrow, maybe, but the other couple!" She babbled on, trying to make small talk, to get Brian to laugh, to bring him into a circle of two. "Why didn't we just take them to one of the American places – Chilli's – or something!" She laughed, but the edges were brittle.

"How can a person be severely allergic to smoke and come to Paris?" he said.

"I wonder how they'll cope with the rest of their trip?"

"Who the hell knows." He let her take his arm as they went down the stairs to the train. "I needed them to stay," he said. "This deal is important, I thought you realized that."

At the bottom of the steps, near the turnstiles and the deserted ticket booth, stood a girl. Candace put her in her early twenties, late teens. She quickly assessed her assets: bouncy, thick blond hair with no split ends; sky-high legs atop running shoes; low-slung hip huggers, revealing a flash of pink thong, tiny slim boy-hips and a white T-shirt, dazzling against creamy tan skin. Candace adjusted her Chanel scarf.

The girl approached Candace and said something in French, something she didn't understand but then she did. The girl wanted to walk through the turnstile with Candace, getting into the Metro without paying. Candace didn't want her to. Definitely not. She said '*Non*,' clearly, and tut-tutted with a wagging finger to make it clear she was not a tourist; she was one who understood the gestures of Paris.

Candace found the petty desire of Parisians to get away with anything they could, annoying and coarse. *Non.* The girl could not make her a party to this picayune crime. A bubble of territorial anger rose in Candace's throat. It was a sour, unpleasant bubble, but it came up so fast she had no time to swallow it. The girl stood her ground and said something in rapid *argo,* clearly insulting. Candace wondered if the girl would push her, or slap her. She was such a tall, fit teen. Candace put her ticket in the little slot and grabbed it as it popped up again. The girl was close behind her. *Non!* she said again. Candace tried to get through quickly but the girl was all around her and too close and she couldn't stop, she was shadowed, the girl was right on her and behind her, and Candace felt the girl's body against *her* body as the girl shoved Candace forward. *NON!* She tried to keep her back but she was pushed forward and she thought *Where is Brian! Why isn't he doing something! He could be so fucking passive sometimes! Damn him!* and she squeezed through the metal doors, the girl directly behind her. She brushed past Candace without a word, just a flick of her perfect blond hair and a flick of her perfect little girl ass high up on long legs.

Candace yelled, *"SALOPE!"* The word hung harsh and hollow. She turned to Brian, who stood a few feet away. "Why didn't you *help*?"

"I wasn't really paying attention," he said with a disapproving frown that exposed the lie.

There was nothing to do but go forward. Candace was close to tears, shaking a little. When they reached the platform, the girl was on the other side. She sat on the orange plastic bench, her head hanging, looking no older than twelve. One foot was twisted sideways and the other rested on it. All the adrenalin of a moment before drained out of Candace into the little trough near the wall where the *clochards* piss. What was a girl that age doing out on the streets of Paris alone at this time of night? Without even any money for a Metro ticket. If there had been a way to turn back time, Candace would have paid a great price, just then, to do so. A train came to the girl's side of the track but when it pulled out the girl had not moved.

"Maybe I should have given her a ticket? Maybe we should see if she's all right?"

"Maybe you shouldn't have called her a bitch," Brian said.

"She shouldn't have pushed me." Candace's cheeks burned.

"I didn't see that," he said.

She let that pass. They'd both agree he didn't see anything. Their train was pulling up.

"Maybe I should go over and apologize," said Candace.

"Maybe you should just let it go, for God's sake," said Brian through his teeth, and he nudged her into the doors. "It's not a big deal."

*Yes, it is.* Candace ducked away from his hand in the small of her back. She didn't want him touching her. He was always nudging her, this way and that. She moved into the car but declined the seat Brian pointed to. He shrugged and sat down. Candace leaned against the doors on the far side. She held her purse in front of her and looked down at her shoes. Her feet hurt. She was afraid she might cry.

"For Christ sake, Candy, it's okay," he said.

"It doesn't feel okay," she said, her shoulders stiff.

She splayed her feet and gripped the handle of her purse tightly. She would not cry. She would not. Brian stared out the window where his reflection stared back at him. As the train picked up speed, Candace caught a glimpse of the young girl. She was approaching a man, her hand out, asking for something.

Candace wanted to call out to her, to say something like, "Get your own!" But that was too cliché, too typical, too completely inadequate. The train began to move. If she had the opportunity, what would she say to a young girl making all the wrong choices? Something, something . . . But it was too late. The train entered the tunnel and they left the fluorescent glare of the station behind. The rails squealed and Candace put her hands over her ears.

# SNOW LIKE SILENCE

Sarah looked up. The sky was whitish, as though the wind had sucked all the blue out of it. She stood at the French doors, gazing into the middle distance of the back garden. She was still in her bathrobe, after her second bath of the day. Geese honked and she raised her eyes in time to catch a glimpse of the migrating birds. Headed north, stupid things. When had she started using the word "things" for every*thing*? Another symptom of menopause? *Oh, please.*

Sarah wanted to do something. She had wanted to do something all day. The question was, what, precisely? And wasn't it always. Arthur, her second husband (although the first marriage had been so short it hardly counted), called her "An Unquiet Soul," in a capital letter sort of way, to make it sound less insulting than she'd always suspected he intended. "Well, Unquiet Soul, what do you want to do?" he'd say, looking over the top of his glasses, over the top of his *New York Times*, over the top of his coffee mug, over his stack of work from the office. Always over the top of something. And she would reply, "Something. I don't know." To which he would sigh and say, "Let me know when you figure it out. I'm at your disposal." Which of course he was not, and then he'd go back to his whatever-it-was and she would fuss around the house, or go for a walk around the neighbourhood, or bake a pie or read the latest must-read book, or buy more scented candles online, though none of these things would be what she wanted to do at all.

*Oh, look, the first snow is falling.* Soft, thick flakes, big as butterflies, fluttered to the grey stone. It stayed on the ground, not melting as most early snows did. She picked out individual flakes, watching them descend from on high until they blended with the mass below. Over and over. Always the same and yet each one purported to be distinct.

With a degree of effort, she shook off the entropy, turned and strode toward the bookshelf. She winced: the recently purchased sisal carpet prickled her feet. It had seemed such a good idea, this redecorating, this move to neutrals, the earthy and serene. Sarah scanned the books. *The Search for Meaning. Living a Purpose-Driven Life. The Cloud of Unknowing. The Key to the Soul.* All bought in the hope that somewhere between their covers was the secret of satisfaction. Her fingernail, polished a translucent shade of petal, trailed the spines. She more or less hoped – hoped more, believed less – that her finger would tingle with a message from her unconscious if she passed the right book, but of course, it did not. Carol, the proudly pragmatic member of *Les Girls*, as her group of friends liked to call themselves, would laugh at her.

The phone rang.

"Hello."

A slight pause.

"Hello, darling."

"How's Paris?" Long distance echo.

"Damp and chill. Dark. Much like London this time of year. But still, it's Paris, isn't it? Beautiful. Elegant. Well-fed. Wish you were here."

"Me, too."

"Really? You could have come. I wanted you to."

"I know. How's the hotel?"

"Nice. I think I saw George Clooney in the lobby."

"Oh, *that* kind of nice."

Pause. Intake of breathe. "You could have come. I thought you were looking forward to some time alone. You did make that clear. Meditation in silence, wasn't it?" And there it was, the little snuffle of hurt in his voice that she so loathed. Why couldn't he just come out and say what he meant? For a man of his size and age – meaning six foot two and fifty-five, surely he should be past pouting and passive-aggressive sniping.

"Yes. Meditation. That was it."

"So, how's that going?"

Ah, the two-week-long hallway of solitude before her, and although she would not tell him, all she felt was ants. Ants under her skin, in her ears, her fingertips.

"It's all right."

"You sound distant."

"I am distant, silly, you're in France."

Silence.

"You could call the girls. One of them would come home for the weekend, or you could go down there."

The girls – in this case their daughters, not *Les Girls* – she knew, would not be persuaded from sunny Florida for anything short of heart attack or house fire. "I'm fine, Arthur."

"I don't think being alone is all that good for you."

"I'm fine, dear. How are the meetings going?" She changed the subject, because she did not want to admit that whatever *was* wrong had only gotten worse since the girls left home. They had always needed one thing or another and had needed it loudly enough to drown out, well . . . It. "Are you going to get the account?"

"Oh, I imagine so. My presentation was good, really good, if I do say so myself . . ." and Arthur droned on about whatever the presentation was, while Sarah thought about her daughters.

The girls were gone now, gone to college, to lives filled with their own needs and wants and pains, all of which they apparently decided were better kept private. Perhaps, Sarah mused, that was her fault. How well did she know Jennifer and Kate, after all? How well had she truly cared to know them? They were such athletic girls, such tall girls, born rowers, Arthur said, just as he had been in college. She picked up a silver-framed photo from the top of the piano, which she no longer played. In the picture, Jenn and Kate, ruddy-cheeked, stood in front of the lake house, laughed with their mouths wide open, their pale fine hair tousled by the wind. At least they had her hair, she thought.

People lived in the same house, you knew their habits, you knew whether they liked their toast buttered cold or warm, whether they slept in pyjamas or nightgowns, but who they were, that was something else, a level of intimacy, for which, she suspected, she had no particular talent. There were just these gulfs, and moments of comfort in between. A warm cheek against yours, a body to curl into at night, a shared laugh, or pain, a glass of ruby wine by firelight.

"Sarah, are you there?" *What had Arthur been saying?*

"Yes, I'm here. I was listening."

"I doubt that."

"Arthur . . ."

Disappointed sigh. "Look, I have to go. I've got some colleagues waiting for dinner."

"Going somewhere nice?"

"Rue Balzac. That singer's place. Johnny Halladay."

"More celebs, then."

"Do you want an autograph?" he laughed.

Of course, he knew how very much she would *not* want an autograph, just as she knew it was precisely the sort of thing he would do, and they both knew that if she were with him it would mortify her. She wanted to leave the conversation on a better note than it began, and so she giggled, almost convincingly, and said, "Oh, yes please."

"I do miss you, Sarah," he said.

"And I miss you, too, darling. Really," she said, and meant that.

"You're all right, then?"

"Yes, dear. I'm fine. I've going to make myself a cup of tea, light a fire and read Virgil."

"Sounds both ambitious and satisfying."

"It's snowing here."

"Is it?"

"It's pretty."

"Well, make sure everything's locked up, won't you?"

"Promise."

"I love you."

"I love you, too. Goodnight. Have fun," she said, and hung up.

Virgil was actually a splendid idea. She could see herself as a woman who curled up in front of the fire with a cup of tea and Virgil. She lit a fire, poured tea, changed into sweatpants and a sweater, thick socks on her feet, and flipped through the book. *I sing of warfare and a man at war. From the sea-coast of Troy in early days/ He came to Italy by destiny . . .*

The snow kept falling. Thicker now. A blanket of quiet descending on the world. She drifted off and dreamed of skating along a frozen river.

When she woke she was hungry and craved something sweet, but considering she'd gained some weight lately and was now firmly in the dress-to-disguise end of her closet, she fixed herself scrambled eggs with smoked salmon and a salad. Outside the window the snow had piled up maybe two, three inches on the top of the birdfeeder. She sat at the counter in the kitchen, but put down a place mat and used the good crystal for a glass a wine. She turned on the local television news. The weather, they said was the big story. A great deal of snow coming, and maybe ice. Stock up, the preternaturally cheerful female anchor said. Get in that firewood.

She heard a shout from outside, went to the front window and looked out at the unplowed street. They lived on an old rural *cul de sac* of only two houses on six acres each. Nothing in front of her own house except a sod field, and they were never in the first or even second tier of the ploughing schedule. Now, children played in the street, four children in the drifts, laughing and throwing snowballs in the dusky light. Three girls and a boy from the looks of it, although it was hard to tell, layered up in jackets and scarves as they were. The oldest, or at least the tallest, pulled the littlest on a silver disk. *What were those things called? Oh yes, flying saucers.* Behind them trudged a man in a great fluffy parka, his hood up, absorbing the snowball hits. She was sure they didn't live on the street, and equally sure they weren't related to the Jacksons, who lived in the other house. How did they get here? Where did they walk from? The man turned toward her, as though he sensed her watching them, and she fought an unreasonable urge to duck behind the curtain. He stood for a moment and she could not be certain, but it seemed he looked directly at her. Sarah suddenly wished she had a dog. And then, as her heart beat too quickly, one of the children hit the man on the side of the head with a snowball and he turned back to the children, roared in mock ferocity, loud enough that she heard him though the closed window, and he pretended to run after them. They shrieked with laughter, yes, laughter, Sarah was sure.

And still, the snow came down. The wind picked up. A swirl of whiteness flew off the roof, like some sort of vaporous devil, and obliterated her view. She wondered about people who got caught in white-outs and froze to death mere feet away from their homes. She decided she wanted another glass of wine.

After dinner, Sarah watched some television, some crime show, or was it two? They ran together and she had trouble figuring out who had done what to whom, or why. She started to doze on the couch in the den, considered sleeping there, since what difference would it make and who would know, but then told herself that a woman who lived a graceful life did not let herself sleep in sweatpants on the couch. Before she went to bed, she did something she did not usually do – she closed all the curtains on the ground floor. As she tugged the drapes, she saw that the snow had stopped. It was raining now, that awful slushy rain that would freeze and make driving impossibly hazardous the next day. All that weather outside made her feel exposed. It was ridiculous, of course, to wonder about the man in the hooded parka. He had been with children. His own children, probably.

All the next day and night and the day following as well, it snowed and rained and snowed and then the snow turned to sleet and began to melt. Arthur called and Jennifer and Kate called and she told them she was just fine, that yes, it was treacherous out there but she wasn't going out there, was she? Snug as a bug, she said. Happy as a solitary clam. Sarah cleaned the house because Maria couldn't get there, of course, and felt tired and virtuous afterward. She watched the news with its endless drone about the dismal weather, and she watched a few old movies and a couple of talk shows, and didn't make much progress on Virgil at all. And then, on the following night, while Sarah slept, the temperature plummeted.

She woke early, to the sound of something cracking. It was barely light and she switched on the bedside lamp, or at least, she turned the switch, but nothing happened. Bulb, she thought, and then, my God, it is so still. She pushed back the covers and put her feet into slippers. The house was cold. She went to the window.

The first slices of pewter crept over the horizon. Everywhere there was silver and crystal. Ice encrusted the trees, the branches hung heavy, the wires sagged. And then she saw it: the oak in the front of the house had split under the weight of ice and snow. She cried out in grief, for it was her favourite tree. It had cracked nearly down the middle, sheered off half the tree. Scattered across the white expanse of lawn, in fact, were all sorts of branches and tree limbs, black as charred bones on the crust of ice that had formed on the snow. It took her a moment to process the extent of the damage. Across the street, or at least where she guessed the street would be, since there was nothing to delineate between that which was road and that which was not, were other trees, similarly mangled. It looked as though some sort of colossal, demented gardener had hacked away at anything in sight, leaving behind only a mess of amputated limbs and deformed trunks. There were holes in the snow, like footprints, deep and regular, but they were not footprints, were they? They were just a bead-line of marks where pieces of trees and hunks of ice had fallen.

She felt slightly dizzy and wondered if she might still be dreaming. Everything seemed so wrong. She looked at the bedside table, at the clock there, to see what time it was, but there were no happy little numbers blinking at her, just a blank black rectangle. She walked to the light switch and flipped it. Nothing. She flipped it again. Nothing. She shivered, and understood.

She would phone Jenn in Florida. Jenn wouldn't be up yet, but Sarah didn't care if she woke her. She needed to know what was going on in the world. She needed a weather report. She picked up the phone and held it to her ear and when she heard nothing at all, she waited like that for a moment, hoping somehow the line would be repaired while she stood. And then she put it down again.

She thought she would take a shower and then decide what to do. By then the power would be back on. Oh, right. No hot water. Well, coffee then. No, no coffee maker. The stove was gas, she could boil water and surely there was instant. Thank God for gas stoves. But then, it struck her that perhaps the gas lines had been damaged, and what would that mean? She ran downstairs, skidded into the kitchen, grabbed matches from the drawer, and turned the knob. Oh, what a beautiful blue flame. And she laughed a little then, to think how she'd panicked.

It was not as though this would last. She would build a fire. She was certainly a woman who could build a fire. She would keep the doors to the den closed so the heat would stay in. She would make soup. There was plenty in the house to eat. She could even warm water to wash in, if the power didn't come back on in an hour or so.

"A woman must maintain standards, after all," she said aloud, in a voice like Katherine Hepburn's, so that she would sound a little silly, and pompous, and it would not seem at all that she was nervous.

When the water boiled and she went to pour some over the instant crystals she had found in the cupboard, she splashed a little on her hand. She jumped, nearly upset the cup, and splashed more. "Shit!" she cried, and ran cold water over the burn. It occurred to her then that something very bad could happen, something very bad indeed, like falling down the stairs or slicing open an artery, and there would be no way to call anyone. She was utterly isolated. Her body would lie on the floor for days before someone would find her. At least, she thought, it wasn't summer. Imagine if the power went out in summer and you lay there in the heat and humidity, with all those flies breeding and your body bloating with gases and decay until . . . Stop. The good news was she'd be frozen and nicely preserved. She dried her hand on a clean dish towel. It was nothing. It wouldn't even blister. Get a grip.

It was the silence. That's what it was. The uncanny silence. It was anticipatory, without even the reassuring hum of a refrigerator. She had never thought of herself as a woman who needed to fill the silence. In fact, she always said she was a woman who longed for silence and solitude. Well, here she was, then, getting exactly what she wanted. What did women in the past do without television and cars and appointments at the spa? They churned butter and wove cloth and spun wool and chopped wood. They worked. Of course, there was that. She could bake bread or do needle-work or heat water on the stove and wash clothes or scrub something. Or, she could have some bread and cheese and read for a while, until the lights came back on, until the snowploughs went through and life returned to normal.

Later, when the fire blazed and she snuggled up under a comforter, she felt very nearly cozy. Her stomach was full and, having tried Virgil again and failed again, she had given in and was reading a surprisingly entertaining mystery by Robert B. Parker. She read for a couple of hours, swept up in the intrigue and the violence, and would have forgotten the weather completely had it not been for having to get up at regular intervals and tend to the fire. Alarming how much wood it consumed. She picked up the nearby phone again, just checking. A dead space so complete it seemed filled with darkness. She put it down again. She wondered if Arthur and the girls had heard about the storm, if they'd tried to call and were worried.

She thought about lunch and went to the kitchen. She was about to open a can of soup when she thought better of it. Best to use up some of the perishables first. Sure, it was cold in the house, but things wouldn't last forever. She opened the freezer and seeing things were still nice and solid, she took out a steak for her dinner and then chose a tub of left-over chilli from the fridge. While it was heating, she decided to go out and get more wood from the side of the house.

She put on extra socks and a scarf and boots and plucked Arthur's jacket from a hook. His old work gloves were in the pocket and she put them on. Carrying the leather wood-tote she stepped into the garage and then realized she couldn't go out that way – the doors were electronically operated and although she was sure there must be a way to open them manually, she didn't know how. She tromped back through the house and went to the front door. She had to push the screen door as snow had drifted up onto the porch and, with the heavy coating of ice, it was an obstinate wedge. There was no path anywhere, of course. Just a crusty whiteness.

"Oh God," she said to the expanse of snow. "I suppose I'm going to have to shovel the walk."

She tried to step off the porch, to see if the ice-crust would hold her. It didn't. She sank through to above her knee. Snow fell into her boot. "Shit."

Get the shovel, then. And begin shovelling. It was hard going. The snow was dense and heavy with ice. She tried banging it down to form a sort of path. She needed sand and salt. She found the bags in the garage, but they were too heavy to carry, so she got a bucket from the laundry room and filled it with a half-and-half mixture. Hauling it back to the front of the house, she felt a draft and realized she'd left the inside wooden door door open. "Idiot," she said. As though she needed more fresh air in here. Which was when she saw the form on the porch through the screen door.

Hooded. A big parka. Dark, hulking as an upright bear. She froze, and tightened her grip on the bucket. Maybe she could hit him on the head with it. It was heavy. It would hurt. He was closer to the door than she was. He would be inside before she could close it. He swiped at his nose with a mittened hand. The other rested on a snow shovel.

"Hello," he said. "You all right here?" His voice was low, with gravel in it.

"Yes." She quickly stepped to the door, got her fingers round the handle. "We are perfectly fine." Let him know she was not alone.

"I got these, see, makes it easy." He pointed at his feet and sure enough, heavy work boots rested on old-fashioned snowshoes, bent wood held together with woven sinew. "My name's Joe Carter. I brought you over some wood from your pile out there."

And it was true; there were five or six logs by the door.

"Thank you," she said.

"Your phones still down?" he asked. He was tall, but with all the padding of that jacket it was impossible to see how big he was, how much was muscle, how much was fat. He was younger than she. His skin the sort of skin that has been outside a great deal, rough and deeply lined, the colour of oak. What was that mark high on his cheekbone, a birthmark? A tattoo? A mole? No, not that shape – like a tear. His teeth, she saw now that he was smiling at her, were small, and very bright in his face, the whites of his eyes faintly yellow. It was a smile, she thought, designed to ingratiate, to disarm, to set at ease, and she did not trust it in the least.

"Are your phones down?" she said.

"All phones are down, I think. You don't hear the news? You don't have a transistor radio?"

"I—" She didn't want to tell him she had no such thing. In fact, other than a flashlight and some extra batteries, she had none of the things you were supposed to have for emergencies. No generator. No rooms full of bottled water. Certainly no rolls of duct tape.

"Reports say this is the biggest ice storm in more than eighty years. All the way through four states. They're bringing the National Guard in, but it's going to take some while, I guess. I think we're on our own here, you know?"

"I'm sure they'll get the power back on soon," she said.

"Hey, maybe, but I think no. You got a fireplace, I see," he pointed up at the chimney where the smoke rose and danced in puffs of wind. "Your chimney good and clean? You don't want a chimney fire, especially when the fire department's out of yelling range."

My God, what was this man, the voice of doom? She had no idea when the chimney had last been cleaned. "It's fine," she said.

"Good. We just moved in a few weeks ago, right? Like *that* was good timing. Down off Quaker Bridge. We call it the igloo."

Sarah knew the house; it had been on the market for ages, vacant for the past two years. Built by hippies back in the early seventies, it was a wooden geodesic dome with leaky skylights scattered around the top and a couple of acres of tick-infested brush.

"You bought the old Snyder place?" She couldn't imagine the Snyders selling to this man, who didn't look like he had enough money for what the land alone would cost, given the way developers were bidding on property. The Snyders had moved to the city to be acupuncturists, and whereas they might have been hippies once, they had become surprisingly avaricious when they learned what others were getting for their battered old properties.

"Renting. Yeah, I know. It's a weird place, but me and Lisa and the kids – we got four – well, it's okay for us. For now." He looked past her into the hall. "You got a nice place."

"I appreciate you bringing me the news . . . Joe, but it's getting cold. Is there anything else?" She tried to sound like a school teacher, someone with authority. Reserved, with good boundaries. She didn't care what he thought of her.

"I saw you, yesterday, when I was with the kids, yeah? You saw me too, right? Well, anyway, I thought maybe you were alone here, and my wife she said I should come over and see if you are all right. I'm going to go up to that other house, too, the one with the old people," he pointed down the street. "I can shovel your walk if you like. This snow is sure heavy. Bring in some wood. Anything you need, like."

"You're looking for work, then?"

His face clouded over and the smile disappeared. "Lady, this is a fucking emergency, you know? Could be days before we get any help. Could be weeks before the power's back on. Christ. I'm not looking for money. I'm looking to help you out."

"I didn't mean anything."

"Yeah, well."

He stared at her until she dropped her gaze, but only for a moment. She looked up at him again, for she must not give him the upper hand. That mark below his right eye. It was a tattoo, a little blue teardrop. She wondered if fear gave off a scent.

"I'm fine, really I am," she said, and then, "Thank you."

"You saw me with my kids."

So, he sensed it then, like a dog, he sensed it.

Her spine stiffened. She wanted to say, how do I even know they're your kids? And what do kids matter? Don't all kinds of sickos have kids? However, that was not the sort of thing you said to a big man with a shovel in his hand.

"They look like nice children."

"They are."

A gust of wind blasted past her, rushed through the house and back out again, bringing with it the smell of chilli singeing.

"I should go. There's something on the stove."

"Oh, you got gas, huh?"

"Yes."

"Lucky you," Joe said, and turned away, moving his feet in wide swings to accommodate the snowshoes. He moved quickly over the top of the snow and ice, sinking in only an inch or two with every step.

Sarah quickly closed the door and locked it, then ran to the window to make sure he was leaving, and to see in which direction he was headed. She cursed herself for never getting a cell phone. Would cell phones work in these conditions? She blew on her hands and thrust them under her armpits, suddenly freezing. Her bones felt cold inside her body, as though she was being frozen from the inside out.

The man lumbered up the white way at a sort of half-run, the momentum of his swinging legs propelling him along. It looked natural to him, as though he were a man used to being in winter woods, and he held the shovel as a hunter might hold a shotgun, in a crooked arm at waist level. His breath came in foggy puffs.

Just then, the old maple across the way let out a mighty creak and then a groan and a crack and the right side split away and fell in a great *thump* that sent up a cloud of debris and snow. The man stopped and then turned back to her house, again seeming to see her through the sheers, as though to say, *You see, I told you it was serious.*

Her chilli was burning. She ran to turn it off, the fumes of scorched meat and beans stinging her eyes, and then ran back to the window. Joe was further up the street but a child, on skis that looked far too small for her, was passing her house now. She wore a bright blue woollen hat and what looked like two or three layers of other children's coats. The rolled-up sleeves revealed mismatched mittens. She laughed and called out, "Dad, Daddy! Hey, Dad!" The man turned and saw her, waved at her, waited for her, his teeth white as the snow, his face bright as the reflected sunlight when he smiled. The child reached him and he leaned toward her so far over his snowshoes he nearly fell, or pretended to, and circled his arms like a cartoon character, pretending to get his balance, which made the little girl laugh some more.

Sarah thought, Oh. Oh, dear.

But surely, the electricity would come back soon.

She put more wood on the fire, got a bowl of chilli, being careful to leave the burned bits on the bottom, and sat by the window, watching. She finished the chilli, and put more wood on the fire. She picked up her book and read a few pages, but was no longer satisfied, or even interested in the murder mystery. Sarah looked out the window, still waiting. Pewter and lead and crystal and all that whiteness, absorbing nothing, reflecting everything. Perhaps this was some new ice age, a great environmental disaster. She thought of lemmings rushing headlong over frozen Arctic cliffs. She was almost out of wood and realized that, interrupted as she had been by the man, Joe, she had not put down the sand and salt, had not made a path to the wood. I am a foolish, pampered woman, she thought, sitting and reading a book while the world freezes.

She hurriedly bundled up and went outside. The days were shorter now; it would be dark by five o'clock. Hours away still, but look at that sky, clouds to the west in a fluffy pattern – it was called a mackerel sky – more snow on the way. A *mackerel sky?* Now where did she pick up that from? Everything else was *thing* this and *thing* that. Maybe crisis sharpened the wits. The snow squeaked under her boots. She looked up the street to see if she could see Joe and his daughter. Perhaps the Jacksons had taken them in. Perhaps there was a problem. They were old, and Edith had a heart problem. Sarah should have gone up to check on them herself. She could still do it. If Joe did not come back by the time she finished with the path, she would go up. Or, perhaps she had missed Joe coming back. Was that possible? She tried to see if there were two sets of tracks in the snow, going up the street and back down, but she couldn't tell. They might have stayed within the same tracks to make the going easier, mightn't they?

It was a long way from the front door to the side of the house and the wood pile. She had wanted to pile it inside the garage, but Arthur said it attracted termites. Fine, but Arthur was not here. Would not be home for days, and only then, she supposed, if the airports were open. Of course they'd be open. She began to work, chipping away at the hard crust, trying to get purchase on the weighty snow underneath. The air was metallic and clean. She dug the blade of the shovel into the snow and hauled with all her might. Grunted with the strain. Managed to heave the clump to the side. Repeated the motion and felt a tiny nip in her shoulder muscle. It was clear she'd never make it. She gave up. She'd just have to tromp and stomp her way through. She stepped heavily onto the ice crust, breaking it on purpose, another step, another, back over the first, the snow over her knees. Her breath was laboured and she was only a quarter of the way there. The only good thing was how warm her exertions had made her. How many trips would she have to make to get enough wood to keep the den warm enough to fend off hypothermia? And then she thought, Oh God, do I even have enough wood? Enough for how many days? It would be easy to panic. Back in 1998, that ice storm in Canada, how may people died? Some were without power for three weeks, weren't they?

She heard the high-pitched squeak of a child's laughter. Joe and his daughter were coming back. Joe held his shovel in one hand and one of the girl's ski poles in the other, pulling her along. She sailed behind him, giggling and shouting, "Go faster! Faster, Daddy!"

As they came closer Sarah waved, but Joe did not wave back and she could not tell if he saw her. "Hello," she called out, which seemed the wrong way to begin, but what else was there? Hey you? "Are the Jacksons all right?" she called.

He slowed but did not stop. The little girl looked at her, with that curious wide-open stare that children have. Her eyes were dark as water-washed pebbles, and her skin was bright in the fresh air.

"Hello, dear," Sarah waved at the little girl. "Joe, did you see the Jacksons?"

"They're fine," he called out, still moving. "For the moment."

"Do they need anything?"

He stopped then, and looked at her. Clearly, she had insulted him. Which rankled her a bit. What did he expect, a strange man at her door? If she was a pioneer woman, she would have met him with a gun.

"They gave us hot chocolate," said the girl. "They have gas." She giggled. "I mean they have a gas stove."

"Oh, isn't that nice. The chocolate, I mean. Not the gas," said Sarah, and the little girl giggled again.

"They don't have all that much wood," said the man. "Enough for a day or two, maybe."

"Surely the power will be back by then."

"You should have a battery radio," he said.

"Have you heard something?"

"National Guard should make it to town tomorrow. Maybe even out here. Or the day after."

"What are they doing?"

"Evacuations."

*"Evacuations?"* She did not want to leave her home. She did not want to go to some school gymnasium somewhere and sleep on a cot with hundreds of other people. She had wood. She had a gas stove. She would be fine until things were back to normal. She was not going to evacuate. They couldn't make her, could they?

"Will you evacuate?"

"We'll have to, probably." He paused and looked at her house, at the smoke coming from the chimney. "The kids can't live on cold soup and baloney."

"But you have a wood stove or something, don't you?"

"Chimney's no good. We'd burn the place down if we had a fire in that thing."

"Oh, dear."

"Maybe we'll go to the old people's house tonight," said the little girl.

"Kelly," the man said in a warning voice. "Quiet."

"But, Daddy— couldn't we?"

"No, Kelly. But we'll check on them in the morning, okay?" And he said something to her softly, which Sarah couldn't hear.

"Oh. Are they that kind of old?" said the girl.

He nodded at Sarah and she could see from the expression on his face that he was angry again. Proud, perhaps. Disgusted with his new neighbours, perhaps. Although he was right about the Jacksons. They were that kind of old. Crotchety and childless, living in a house full of porcelain figurines and white sofas. "You take care," he said, and began to move off.

"Joe, actually I could use your help," she said before she was completely sure it was what she wanted to say.

"You actually could, huh? Well, I got to get back and check on my wife and kids. Sorry." And then he stopped, tucked the ski pole under his arm and wiped at his face. "Look, I'll try and get back later, okay?"

"Your family can't sleep there tonight if there's no heat. You'll all freeze."

"We'll be all right. We got sleeping bags. It's like camping, right Kelly?"

"I have to share a bag with Annie," she said, her face a little thunderstorm underneath the blue hat. "She kicks. And she has gas. Not the stove kind."

"Oh, well, then," said Sarah. "I think I have an extra sleeping bag or two. We could each have our own, couldn't we? And we could sleep in front of the fireplace. It might be fun. Joe, do you think your wife would mind moving up here for a little while?" A woman she hadn't met. Four children. A man with a tattoo on his face. *Les Girls* would be horrified. Albert would have a fit. And then she was afraid again, but sometimes you just were, weren't you? And you did things anyway, and that's what changed other things.

Things, things, things, books and carpets and clothes and paintings and old photos and her mother's silver candlesticks and that emerald ring Arthur bought her for her last birthday. On and on. Three floors of this house full of things. Too many things altogether. In for a penny . . . "If worst comes to worst, I think there's even a chainsaw in the garage – and some extra gas." There you go, put a chainsaw in this man's hands. "We could cut wood, couldn't we? There's enough of it lying around." She gestured at all the broken branches, the trees that surely never would survive this. "And we can cook here."

"We're a lot of people. The kids are a handful. And, well, we have a dog."

"I'm very fond of dogs," she said, laughing a little at the thought of how Arthur would just have to take antihistamines for his allergies when he returned. "I'm sure we could manage." Although she was not at all sure. How could anyone be sure of anything in a world that froze overnight and changed everything?

"It's good of you."

"I'll feel safer if you're all here, frankly." She smiled. "My husband, Arthur, he's away on business. I don't know when he'll get back now."

"I figured you were on your own." He thought for a moment. "All right then. I'll get Lisa and the kids. We'll come back. We've got some food. I'll bring that." He wiped at his face again. "Can't tell you what—"

"Oh, that's lovely. I'll be most grateful," said Sarah, before he could continue.

He began to move away and then stopped. "Hey," he said, "I don't know your name."

"It's Sarah."

By five o'clock it was dark and snowing again. The snow fell, and kept falling. All around, snow like silence wafted into drifts around the corners of the house, into the nooks and alcoves of the house. The night wandered in, as night in the city never does, without the resistance of a single light bulb or street lamp. Sarah stood, with a blanket around her shoulders, watching from the front window. Waiting. Across the coverlet of snow, the battered black-spined trees were just visible. It was so quiet Sarah heard only her own breathing and the sigh of wind, the creak of the house settling into itself, the soft clump of snow tumbling from the eaves. She watched and watched and waited, all the while the snow gathering in drifts, obliterating any path she had tried to make to the wood pile. That unfinished path. There was very little wood left in the house. Enough for another hour or two, perhaps. And still, she waited, but no one came. Perhaps they decided to use the stove after all. Perhaps something had happened to one of the children. Perhaps the National Guard had made it to their house and evacuated them. Perhaps he had never intended to come, punishing them all for her suspicious mind. She turned off the gas underneath the pot of stew. She resumed her post at the window, the ghostly light on her face turning her into a shadow by firelight.

At last, she had no choice but to bundle up again and wade through the snow, searching for wood like that poor man in the Christmas carol, gathering winter fuel. It had seemed so quaint when she sang it. Where was her good King Wenceslas? It was frigid and the tears on her face crystallized before falling. She had to knock snow off the woodpile and the logs seemed heavier for being frozen. She fell twice and scraped her chin on bark the second time, calling out in frustration, the words whipped back into her mouth by the wind. She only managed three logs. There would have to be many more trips if she was going to keep even moderately warm through the night. On her third trip, when her fingers were numb and her breath broken glass in her throat, without warning the snow stopped and the sky changed and she stood by the wood pile, her boots full of melting slush, and watched until the world was nothing but dark and silver moonlight and the snow settled everywhere like a dream of silence. It seemed as though someone had suddenly stopped speaking, just as they were about to tell her something terribly important.

# THE PRETTY

John eased the battered brown Cadillac into the gravel driveway. It rattled and shook in the potholes and clouds of dust billowed in the open windows. Helen flapped her hands in front of her face and wished, not for the first time, that this clunker had air conditioning. And seat belts. They followed the drive until they saw the house and then parked. John glanced over at Helen, looking for a reaction. He knew the way the place must look to her, with the old spring-sprung La-Z-Boy on the sagging porch and the scrubby yard, but it was important she see where he came from. He was thinking what a difference it would make, having her understand him. She tried to keep her face impassive. She was thinking she would get through this day and be a lady about it. Tomorrow, it would all be over.

John's seventeen-year-old brother Petey was working in the noonday heat, tinkering on an old Camero.

"Hey, Johnny! Who you got in there?" Petey shaded his eyes and peered in the windshield. "Well, fuck me," he said, staring at Helen.

"How you doing, kid?" John said as he got out, the door creaking on its damaged hinges. He leaned against the car, crossing his cowboy boots at the ankle, and his arms across his chest. Helen opened the heavy door, pushing hard, and stepped out, turning both legs toward the door first so as not to give Petey a view of that which he was so plainly hoping to see. She smoothed her tight denim skirt over her hips, adjusting the white eyelet band around the hem where it had crumpled under her thighs.

She looked at Petey and had trouble believing he was John's brother. Petey was softly, poke-ably, overweight, and not as tall as John, who was lean and hard, his thighs long under worn jeans.

"This is Helen, Helen Elworth," John said. "We're seeing each other now."

Petey wiped his hands on an oil rag and stuck his arm out. He was sunburned and the skin peeled across his stubby nose.

"Pleased to meet you," he said. "You sure are pretty."

Helen shook his hand and willed herself not to look at her palm to see if there was dirt on it. When John had asked her to come with him and meet his family, she'd agreed on a whim because she was curious. It might be fun, and John was sweet. She thought it would do his reputation good to have a girl like her on his arm. What better good-bye gift could she give him?

John had been the perfect solution to the Danny Problem – Danny who had lurked outside the boutique, crying and pleading whenever he saw her. John was big and strong and exactly the sort of man who liked to come to the rescue of a lady in distress. It had never been Helen's intention to lead him on and she was definitely going to tell him thanks and good-bye after this weekend. She'd worked hard to get out of where she'd come from. She was going to marry a stockbroker or a doctor. Not a guy like John, who supervised a loading dock. Not a guy whose family lived in a ramshackle old place like this, or who had a car up on blocks in the front yard.

"Nice to meet you," she said to Petey.

"Mom and Dad home?" said John.

"Mom is," said Petey, still staring at Helen. "Dad's down at the hotel."

"Come on, sugar," John said, coming around to Helen and taking her hand, "let's go inside."

Petey followed them, and stood in the doorway, scuffing his shoe wordlessly on the grimy brown kitchen tiles. The kitchen was dark, even in the noonday sun, and it was not particularly clean. Dishes were piled in the sink. Cereal lay scattered on the counter. An ashtray spilled butts on the sticky-looking checked oilcloth covering the table.

John's mother stood with her head in the refrigerator, bent over, her wide backside stretching the blue-flowered fabric of her housedress. She turned when she heard the screen slam, a baloney roll in one hand. When she saw John and Helen, her other hand automatically flew up to the three pink sponge curlers on her head, one over each ear, and one over her forehead.

"Johnny! Why didn't you tell me you was coming up and bringing company!" She pulled the curlers.

"Didn't want you to go to a bunch of trouble, Mom. Thought I'd just surprise you." John gave her a big hug, picking her up off the ground.

"Put me down, you idiot, and introduce me to your girl!"

"Mom, this is Helen Elworth," he said, putting her down gently. "Helen, this is my Mom."

"How do you do, Mrs. LaSalle?"

"Well, sure is nice to meet you, honey. You staying?"

"Naw," said John. "We gotta go back tonight. Helen owns a store. Real nice ladies' clothes. She's gotta open up in the morning."

"Runs a store, did you say? Well, ain't that something." Kitty looked Helen up and down, her eyes openly hungry as she took in Helen's pink-flowered blouse, the flounced denim skirt and her tiny waist, circled by a creamy yellow belt. "Look at you, matching yellow shoes and all. Where'd you find shoes that colour? You know, I saw a sweet little skirt like that down at the Wal-Mart. Course, I could never fit into it, but you sure got the figure for it."

Helen wanted to tell her she was sure that a store as low-class as Wal-Mart would *not* be carrying an outfit like hers, but John's mother went on talking before she had a chance.

"You kids want some lunch? I'm just fixing to make up some sandwiches for Petey and me. You want a baloney sandwich? Or I got olive loaf? Maybe you like that better?"

"To be honest, Mrs. LaSalle, a glass of iced tea is all I can manage in this heat."

"You call me Kitty, honey. Everybody calls me Kitty."

Helen looked at the ham-fisted woman, her thighs like slabs of pork, her nose a turned up snout, and her hair frizzing out in tufts. "That's a sweet name, Kitty. It suits you," she said, and the woman grinned.

"Now, you can't live on iced tea! You let me fix you a plate, maybe some tomatoes from the garden and some lettuce. I'll bet a little city girl like you lives on salad." She turned back to the refrigerator. "Petey, get us some plates."

"You're just gonna have to eat something," said John. "She's not going to give up until you do." He held his hands up helplessly.

She ate, with a smudgy knife and fork, a piece of beige meat spotted with green olives, a few leaves of pale lettuce, a blood-red tomato, and a slice of white bread. She gulped sweet iced tea to take away the musty taste. Kitty LaSalle hovered over her, asking if she wanted more of this, more of that. It took repetition to persuade the woman that she was full, truly, quite full. She dabbed her lips with a paper napkin and tried to smile.

John stuffed his mouth with a meat sandwich as though trying to eat as quickly as possible. The mustard squeezed out of the bread and caught at the corners of his mouth. When he was finished, he leaned back on a battered chair, balanced precariously. His legs were spread wide and his hands lay on his hips, thumbs tucked in his pockets.

"Feel like going for a drive?" he said. "We could go find Dad."

Helen was anxious to be anywhere but here. This kitchen stirred up memories of her childhood kitchen, her own mother, fat and unhealthy, with an ever-present cigarette dangling from her bloodless lips. She wished John wouldn't sit like that. Her eyes kept trailing to his hips, his legs, the thick package of his sex.

Petey made a wettish noise, pushed open the screen door and spit over the porch rail.

"Yes," said Helen, "let's go for a ride."

The car was hot from sitting in the sun, the vinyl seats like an iron under their thighs. They drove with all the windows open and Helen's thick coffee-coloured hair flew in the breeze.

John drew her close to him, his arm around her shoulders, oblivious to the heat. Helen squirmed under his arm. She trapped her hair in her hand so it wouldn't blind him as he drove. He was filled up inside with things he wanted to explain to her.

"You got hair like one of those shampoo commercial girls, you know that?" he said.

"Bottled water," she said.

"Huh?"

"I rinse my hair in bottled water. It keeps it shiny."

He thought of her with her hair all wet and sticking to her skin, and he reached his hand under her arm to her breast.

"Don't, John," she said, but she didn't move away. His hand was calloused from work and yet his touch was feather light on the thin material of her blouse. A shiver ran from her arm all the way down her hip. "Don't," her voice lower.

It was a fifteen-minute drive to town, to the McInley Hotel. By the time they got there, Helen's face was flushed and her breathing shallow. As he parked under the shade of an oak tree, she slid away from him.

"We don't have to go in," he said. "We could go up to Belle Lake."

"Don't be silly," she said. "We have to see your father."

"You glad you came?" he asked her. He shifted in the seat, pulling at the crouch of his pants, trying to ease his erection.

"Yes, of course."

"You don't seem too thrilled."

"It's hot, is all."

They sat in the parking lot under a shade tree. He wasn't used to women keeping him at arm's length. "I thought your coming up here with me meant something."

"I told you I'd come because you wanted me to, John. And because I had no other plans for this particular Sunday." She patted fresh powder on her face.

"It means something to me," he said. "More than just a way to fill up your free time," he said. "You understand that, right?"

"Of course, don't worry, it'll be fine," she said, thinking of his reputation. She smiled brightly. "Shall we go in?"

They got out of the car and John led her in, holding her hand. The hotel was not much of a hotel. It was mostly a bar and pool hall. In the evenings, they had third-rate country singers and Saturday night was the big night. In the unforgiving light of Sunday afternoon, the toll of such success was obvious. The carpet was scattered with cigarette burns and a mosaic of unidentifiable stains, some of them the dark brown of blood. It smelled musty, of old smoke, sweat, and beer. Three men in John Deere baseball caps sat at the bar. They each had a bottle of Bud and a shot glass in front of them. They looked alike: sunburned and leathery, with watery eyes. They wore the same saggy jeans, slung low over their bellies. Two wore short-sleeved shirts, faded pale from much washing, and the third, whose face was badly marked with acne scars, wore a too small T-shirt. It rode up in the back, exposing the upper part of his buttocks.

There were wooden tables, scuffed and covered in water-marks, at uneven intervals around the room. Four women sat at one, wearing stretch pants and loose blouses, their hair piled high and dyed bright colors. Now and then, they let loose with shrill laughter and one of them pounded the table with the palm of her hand.

Travis Tritt's voice came over the juke-box "*. . . I start to think I'm ten feet tall and bullet-proof . . .*" The crack of pool balls came from somewhere in the back.

"Ain't much, is it?" said John, as they stood in the entrance. "I don't mind visiting, but I couldn't ever live here again." He wanted to tell her more, that he'd had his heart broken for the first time on the porch of this very hotel, that he got drunk for the first time here, that he got laid for the first time upstairs in room 6 with Christie Clark who had three kids now and was divorced twice.

The look on her face made him wish he'd never brought her here at all. She looked like she had a small dead fish under her nose. She was missing the point. She was too standoffish by far. Thought she was so fine. His jaw tensed.

She noticed him clench his teeth and assumed he was ashamed.

"Well, no bar really looks good with the lights on, does it?" she said. She wanted to be kind. She put her hand on his arm. "Do you see your Dad?"

"He'll be in the back room." Without waiting to see if she was following, he walked across the room.

"Hey, Johnny-boy!" called out the man in the middle of the bar trio. How's it hanging, kid?"

"Doing fine, Fred, doing fine," he said, without stopping, and vanished around the corner of the bar.

She trotted after him, ignoring the stares. The back room opened up to a larger space, with big windows overlooking a parking lot. Two pool tables occupied most of the area, and along one wall was another bar, with neon signs advertising various beers above it. There were tables along the windows, a rack for pool cues, and a plastic sliding scorekeeper. Two men stood lolling against their cues, a third sat with his cue between his legs and an empty glass in his hand. The fourth man, thin and hollow-chested, but with such a resemblance to John that there was no doubt he was his father, leaned far over the green felt table, his eye in a squint, sighting the cue ball. *Clack!* The shot rang true and the ball, faster than the eye could follow it, smacked into the eight ball, which bounced first off one rail, then the other, and sped surely to the corner pocket.

"Yeah! That's the way to do it, boys!" called out the thin man.

"Might as well just let you cash our cheques directly, Burt. Son of a bitch!" said one of the three, who wore a pair of overalls and a camouflage hunting-cap. He, and the other two, peeled bills out of their pockets and slapped them down on the bar.

"Look what the cat's dragged in!" said the seated man, biggest of the four. He must have been three hundred pounds, his eyes buried in pools of fat.

"Hey, Dad," said John, "Harry, Dave, Buck." He nodded to each in turn.

"Hey, Johnny!" His father came around the table. Both men opened their arms and gave each other a backslapping. Burt LaSalle barely came up to his son's shoulder. "Didn't know you were coming down. Where you been the last few months?" He erupted into a lung-ripping cough. John waited until he caught his breath.

"Just been busy, you know, work and all."

"Yeah, I can see that," said the older man, looking at Helen, who stood waiting in the doorway. He pulled a pack of cigarettes from his shirt pocket and tapped one out. "Who's this pretty young lady?"

"This is Helen."

Burt lit a cigarette, which triggered off another coughing fit.

"Jesus, Dad, why don't you give 'em up?"

"Only thing that keeps me breathing," he chuckled. "Come here, girl, let's get a look at you."

Helen stepped forward, her hands folded in front of her. She smiled tentatively. "Nice to meet you, Mr. LaSalle."

"Mr. LaSalle? Jesus, get a load of that, boys," he turned to the men, who now stood at the bar drinking from fresh beers. "*Mister* LaSalle!" He cackled and coughed. "You want to fit in around her, darlin', you'll have to learn to drop the formality. Burt'll do!" Before she could react, he stepped in and gave her a rib-cracking hug. She squealed and the men laughed.

"Don't break her, Dad," John said.

"Hell, I'm not hurting you, am I, Helen?"

"No, of course not." She smiled at John, to show she was a good sport.

"Have a drink. Roy, get them a drink. Beer for John. What do you want, honey?" he asked her.

"An ice tea would be lovely."

"Ice tea? That all? Can't have just ice tea. Put a shot in it, Roy. No, make it one of them Long Island ice tea things the kids drink. Sure."

"Oh, I don't think so."

"No point in arguing with Dad. Trust me," John smiled sheepishly. He leaned towards her, whispered in her ear, "You don't have to really drink it if you don't want it, just sip it."

"Fine," she said.

Burt ushered them to a seat near the window and brought them the drinks. "Go on, drink up," he said. "Cheers." He raised his glass, and they raised theirs and clinked. Helen took a sip. It didn't taste strong. And she was so thirsty in this heat. She drank some more.

"What's happening at the plant, Dad?" said John.

"Oh, same old crap," said Burt, and began to explain what was wrong with the fucking union and why he should have been elected shop steward, if the fix hadn't been in. Helen tried to listen, but soon grew bored and looked out the window.

In the back of the parking lot, a silver trailer baked in the sun, heat waves pulsing all around it. A black and grey mongrel dog lay panting under the homemade steps. Someone had rigged up a wash line between two trees and a mouldy-looking red plaid sleeping bag hung across it to air. The scene depressed her but she couldn't take her eyes off the dog, thinking he would surely cook under the oven of the trailer.

The back of her thighs stuck to the chair and she tried to lift them, discreetly, so they wouldn't be all red. Why didn't they have any air conditioning in this place? What a dump. She sipped some more of the cool drink. It reached into her muscles and loosened them. She began to relax and scanned the room. *Tacky room. Tacky town. Tacky people. Tacky bar.* It was sad really, because John was so appealing. A few years ago, she might have let herself be lured by his gentle, protective ways and his beautiful shoulders, but not now. She'd come too far. Well, she could put up with it for the rest of the day, put a good face on it. At least she knew now. It simply would not do, as the characters in the British novels she liked to read would say.

"What's so funny, sweetheart," said Burt. She hadn't realized she'd been smiling. He was looking at her with an odd expression, which she might think was dislike if she did not know better.

"Oh, nothing, really. What were you saying?"

"You know, John," said Burt, ignoring Helen again, "you should come back up next week; we're going up to Sparrow Lake. Gonna go bass fishing. Me and Eddie and your cousin Lloyd. You like fishing, Helen?"

"Pardon me?"

"I said, you like fishing?"

"No, I don't suppose I do."

"Now see, I took you for a fishing girl. You've got that quiet way about you."

"Well, I've never been fishing."

"You don't say. We could fix that, couldn't we, John?"

"I don't think Helen'd like fishing, Dad."

"Looks like a girl handy with a worm to me," he winked, "bigger the better, I figure." And he laughed until he coughed and kept on coughing.

"Is he all right?" said Helen, her hand over her mouth and nose.

"He'll be fine. Just smokes too damn much," said John, but he looked worried.

"I'm going to the ladies' room," said Helen as she stood up.

Burt got his hacking under control, spitting into a plaid handkerchief. He watched Helen's tidy figure as she left the room.

"She sure is pretty," he said.

"Yeah, ain't she?" said John, taking a swig of his beer.

"She's not for you, though."

John wiped his mouth. "What're you talking about?"

"That one thinks she's too good for the likes of you."

"You don't know what you're talking about. She's just shy."

"She's stuck-up. You remember, boy, pretty is as pretty does."

"She's a real hard worker. She's trying to make something of herself."

"She's trying to run from herself, that's what she's up to."

"You think you got the whole world figured out, there behind your beer bottle?"

"No point in getting mad at me, boy. I'm just looking out for you. If she's what you want, it's fine with me, but you won't be happy."

"Let's just change the subject, okay?"

"Fine with me," said Burt.

"Fine," said John.

"What's fine?" said Helen, who walked back to the table, looking fresh and clean and smelling of roses.

"Why, you are, sugar," said John, kissing her on the cheek.

They ordered another round of drinks, and the afternoon slipped away. People came and went, and Helen was introduced to all of them. She tried to be charming, she really did, but it was tiring. She liked the way people looked at her, though, the men admiringly, the women either shy or hostile. It softened her feelings toward John. She felt good, doing something nice for him like this. And it made her proud, the way they looked up to her.

Finally, John suggested they call home, grab a pizza and head back to the house. Helen's stomach rumbled. She had not realized how hungry she was. Usually she never ate pizza, but maybe just this once, she said, with extra cheese and pepperoni? The men laughed and Burt said, "Anything the little lady wants."

By ten o'clock the air in the small battered kitchen was thick with cigarette smoke. The light was dull, hazy, and night bugs made fluttering patterns of shadow as they smashed into the window screens. At irregular intervals, they sizzled against the bulb over the door on the porch and their bodies, heavy now wing-bare, "tocked" against the step. A dozen or more flies hung like tiny smoked hams from a twisted strip of paper on the kitchen ceiling.

They drank Corona beer without the limes. Helen drank hers from a glass. The table was littered with overflowing ashtrays and potato chip crumbs and empty bottles. They had exhausted what little conversation had ever existed between them, and they stared dully at their beer or at their fingers pulling labels off the bottles.

"I suppose we should be leaving soon," said Helen. "Don't you think, John?"

"We can stay another hour. I'll still have you home by midnight."

"Do you think we could move out onto the porch, maybe? It's awful smoky in here."

"You don't want to do that," said Burt, in his phlegm-thick voice. "You would get eaten up with 'skeeters." He coughed, and pounded himself with a grey fist on his breast-bone.

"And black flies," said Kitty. "Don't forget those little bastards. You'd think they use a knife and fork, the size of the chunks they take out of you." She popped her half-smoked cigarette into her beer bottle, where it fizzled out in the quarter inch of amber liquid.

Helen looked around the darkening room. Petey was in the next room, watching *America's Most Wanted,* craning his neck around the door jamb, trying to look under the table, and up her skirt. She stuck her tongue out at him.

"You want another beer, honey?" said Kitty.

"No. Honestly. You've been very kind. But I really think we should be going. Don't you, John?"

"Well, I guess." He hoped she wanted to leave because she wanted to be alone with him. He sure wanted to be alone with her. "Yeah, we should be going."

They made their hurried good-byes, and she turned her head away when Petey hugged her, so that his wet lips only grazed her cheek. Kitty insisted she take a basket of tomatoes with her.

"You make sure you bring her back now, John," said his mother.

"Yeah," said Petey, "soon."

"You bet," said John.

"Thanks for everything," she said. "Sure was nice meeting you."

"I think John's found a real nice girl," Kitty said to her husband, waving as the car pulled out.

"Uh-huh," he said, and tossed his cigarette butt onto the gravel drive.

Driving down the winding road that led to the highway, John itched to get the words out. He started first one sentence, then another, but they were all wrong.

"Come here," he said, at last. He put his hand on her thigh and urged her toward him.

"Just drive, John." The heat, the pizza and the alcohol had made her groggy and faintly ill.

"What's the matter with you?" He quickly took his hand away.

"Nothing."

"Look, I was thinking. We don't have to go back tonight. We could stay around here someplace, and leave early in the morning. I could get you to work on time."

"I don't think so."

"It could be romantic, you and me. I know a real nice little inn."

"No."

"You can't keep pushing me away like this, Helen. I want this thing to move forward, you know what I mean?" She didn't answer.

They were nearing a picnic spot. He slowed the car and pulled in.

"Why are we stopping?" she said.

"I want to talk to you."

"Oh, John, I'm tired. Please just take me home."

"Look at me, Helen." He reached over and put his hand under her chin. Turned her face to him. "I don't think this trip was such a good idea after all."

"Why do you say that?"

"Well, I wanted to show you who I was, where I came from, you know?"

"You have a lovely family."

"Bullshit. We're just a trashy no-account poor bunch of peckers. I know that. Don't think I don't know that." His voice rose.

"Okay. Don't get worked up."

"Come *here*," he said again. He pulled her to him. He put his lips on the side of her neck, where the hollow of her collarbone smelled like baby powder and roses. She shivered. He let his tongue lick softly along her skin. He heard her take a quick gasp of air and felt her muscles go limp.

"I want you to know me, sugar, know that I'm going to make something of myself."

"Uh-huh." Her head tilted back. He covered her mouth with his, parting her lips with his tongue, slowly, softly. He was so good at this. Surely it wouldn't matter, if she let him, just once . . .

"I need you to understand me, how we're alike, you and me," he murmured between kisses. His hand moved to her shoulder, her breastbone, smooth as porcelain, to her breast, the nipple achingly hard. She arched her back, moving toward his hand, but he teased her, his fingers just barely touching her. She moaned, tried to press against him.

"Peas in a pod, you and me," he said.

"What?" She was drugged, sleepy.

He took her nipple between his fingers and rolled it back and forth. He put his other arm around her and cradled her, moved his hand down her belly, across her thighs, to the hem of her dress. His tongue flicked across her lips.

"You don't have to put on airs with me, baby girl, I can tell." His hand slipped under her dress and her legs parted slightly. He felt heat there. "We come from the same kinda history, and together we can break out."

Her hand clamped down on his wrist.

"What?!"

Startled, he drew his head back.

"What're you talking about? We're not anything alike!" she said, sitting up straight.

"It's okay," he said, reaching for her again, trying to bring his mouth to her mouth, "I understand."

"You don't understand anything! What on earth gave you the impression I come from anything like *that?*" She laughed, jagged and rough. "My family's nothing like that! I couldn't ever bring you home to meet them. Don't you understand that?"

John sat up, felt his erection wilt. "When are you going to give it up, Helen? All this hoity-toity crap. You don't fool anyone. Your rough edges are showing. Real class women don't put little flowers in their manicures, or wear all them imitation gold chains . . ."

"Shut up! What would you know about it?"

"I know that much. You think you're such hot shit working in that cheap little boutique? Let me tell you, sweetheart, it ain't no George Armani!"

"*Giorgio*, you idiot!"

"Whatever! And I know a real lady wouldn't treat a man like you do. You aren't nothing but a little prick tease, you know that?"

"I want to go home! Right now. You take me home, John LaSalle!"

"You want to go home? Fine!" He revved the engine and spun out of the rest area, spitting gravel out behind the car. They drove for several miles in silence.

"You are some bitch," he finally said.

"You know, I was going to tell you I was through with you anyway," she said, examining the back of her hands, ensuring she hadn't broken a nail in the tussle. "You've just proven how right I am. You're low class, John. I must have been crazy to ever have anything to do with someone like you in the first place." She flipped the visor down and checked her makeup in the mirror, running a finger along her lower lip. "And to have you think we have anything in common. With a trashy background like yours. It's laughable." And she tried to laugh, but couldn't quite pull it off.

Without warning, he pulled the car off the main road and onto the old logging track. The car fishtailed in the dirt and it took him a moment to get it back under control. Helen braced herself on the dashboard. He drove fast and thought about her smooth pale skin, polished with expensive creams and smelling of sandalwood and rose.

"What are you doing, John?"

He didn't answer. Drove deeper into the darkening wood.

"For Christ sake, John, don't be dramatic. Turn the car around," she said slowly, letting the words droop at the ends, as though talking to an errant child.

He told her to shut the fuck up, just shut the fuck up and he didn't turn the car around, he kept on driving, be-cause he would have her, in the mud and the wet rotting leaves. He would have her, by God, this woman who thought she was so fine. His blood grew thick with the knowledge of what he was about to do.

"John. Stop this." Her voice was edgy now, higher, and squeakier. He looked over at her and saw the fear in her eyes.

He was panting. Like a dog he was panting. He heard his own ragged breathing, smelled the stink of something ani-mal. His hands gripped the wheel, tight as claws, wanting to tear something. He looked at his hands; saw them as things disconnected, with a primitive life of their own. He had always been proud of his hands, and what they could accom-plish.

"Ah, fuck it," he said. "Just fuck it."

He slammed the brakes on and the heavy car skidded to a stop. The headlights showed the churned up road-dust like smoke swirling all around them.

"I want to go home," she said, and her voice was small.

He hit the wheel so hard she felt the tremors all the way to her side of the car.

"I swear to God, Helen, if you say one more word, just one fucking word, I will kick your skinny ass out of this car and you can fucking walk back to the city." His voice was low and constrained, because he spoke through bared teeth.

It took him some time to turn the car around. He had to inch his way this way and that, backwards and forwards. The road wasn't wide and he didn't want to end up in the ditch. There's no telling what might happen if he found himself stuck out here with her, so far from where anyone could hear them. At last, he managed it and drove back to the main road. She was as silent as if he had gagged her.

The lights along the side of the road became more frequent, and soon they came to a gas station. He pulled into the parking lot.

"Get out," he said.

"Here?" She looked around, but there was nothing but the gas station. It was little more than a booth with a skinny kid inside, his face covered with acne, smoking a cigarette.

"Get out."

"You can't leave me here!?"

"Bus'll be by in about an hour. Take you to the city." He reached in his pockets and handed her thirty dollars. "This'll pay for your fare and a taxi from the depot in town." He leaned across her body, and she pressed back, lifted her hands up as though something dirty was passing by. He opened the door.

"Get out."

"Can't you just drive me home?"

"Get the fuck out, I'm telling you, for the last time, you need to get out of this car!" His face was stone and his eyes shone with a dark flame.

"You're crazy, John LaSalle. Crazy!" There was an edge of panic in her voice, which he found more appealing than her usual nasal superiority.

"No, I ain't. But I sure as hell have been. Hey, maybe some guy'll come along and you can tell him all about the cruel man who left you by the side of the road. That's your style ain't it?" He gave her a shove and she recovered just before she toppled onto the asphalt. As she scrambled for footing, he tossed her purse out after her and shut the door.

"You can't leave me here!"

He pulled the car back onto the road, relief flooding into his blood. He wasn't going to end up in jail for her. There were lots of girls with pretty skin, pretty eyes, and pretty legs. He looked in the rear-view mirror. She stood at the side of the road. She stamped her foot and waved her fist at him, the middle finger raised high. The heel of one of those pretty yellow shoes she set such store in was broken and she leaned at an awkward angle. He couldn't help it, he laughed.

# NEIGHBOURS

On Tuesday evening, Bob Yates, who everyone called Big Bob, rambled from room to room in the tidy little house. His wife, Cindy, followed him and begged him not to do anything stupid.

"Isn't one death in the family enough?" she said. "You want me to be a widow, too?" She twisted a dishtowel in her hands. "You don't love me, is that it? Because that's what it means, you know. It's the only thing that explains why you'd want to do something so . . ." and here she paused, her face like a crumpled tissue, ". . . so suicidal!"

He wanted to reach out, take her pale freckled face in his hands, and brush her fine red hair away from her forehead. He wanted to look into her swollen eyes, the lashes so pale, and tell her everything would be all right. However, clearly, that would be a lie, since God had proven without a doubt that things would never be all right again, that there was no compassion in the weft and weave of things.

"I'm begging you, Bob," she said, over and over, "don't do anything crazy."

He looked at her, this woman he loved.

"You know what we are?" he said, gazing at the three porcelain mallards forever migrating on the wall between the den and the kitchen. "We are ducks in the shooting gallery of God's carnival."

"How fucking poetic," she said, and the look on her face was something very much like hatred.

He wanted to be able to comfort her, take her in his arms, but they wouldn't move. He didn't mean to hurt her; he wanted to do something to stop her from hurting. In fact, that was the intent of his plan, to do something that would lance the boil of pain festering on both their souls. She would see that. For now, though, it was best she believe he had set the plan aside.

Earlier that same Tuesday evening, when he'd been out oiling up his old Remington, she'd come searching for him. She'd taken one look, seen what he was doing, turned on her heel and walked back into the house without a word. Bob's father had given him the gun for his twelfth birthday, for hunting squirrels. He'd hardly ever used it and it was stiff with neglect. Big Bob had shot a squirrel just once, and, seeing the horrific aftermath of what a bullet did to such a fragile life, had wept over the twitching bundle of fur and blood. The unalterable finality of the act had appalled him. He shot at cans for a while, because his father seemed to require that he be a good shot, but at last, with much relief, had put the gun back in its flannel wrap, zipped up the canvas bag, and put it away. And so it had lain, locked in a steel case in the basement, until today.

When he'd finished polishing, cleaning and making the gun ready, he walked into the house where Cindy stood waiting for him, her jaw twitching with all the backed-up words.

It was past ten now, and Big Bob and Cindy had been going around like this for hours. They were both exhausted, had *been* exhausted, it seemed, forever. Just swinging your feet to the side of the bed, brushing your teeth, or opening a can of tuna could bring tears to your eyes. No one ever said how tired grief made you.

"I can't take any more, Bob. I'm gonna crack wide open. You have to promise me." She looked as though whatever puppet master held her strings would let go at any moment and she'd crumple to the floor. "Promise me," she said. A tear dripped from her chin.

"Nothing's going to happen tonight. You don't have to worry," he said, which was not what he wanted to say. He wanted to say *I love you and I will make this better and I will make something good come out of this nightmare and please, baby, please have a little faith in me.* What he said was, "Go to bed. I'll be up in a few minutes."

She shook her head and what little strength she had seemed to leave her. She did as he told her, and went to bed. She climbed the stairs heavily, pushing the rock of her mourning before her. After a few minutes, Bob heard her crying, then slowly, the sobs subsided and she whimpered in her sleep.

For an hour or so Big Bob stood on the front porch, leaning up against the yellow post. The paint was peeling and he flicked a flake off onto the dry lawn with his thumbnail. He and Todd had been going to repaint the place this summer, but he'd have to do it alone now. Or maybe he'd just let the place peel and blister away until there wasn't anything left but a shadow on a vacant lot.

For a week after the funeral, neighbours had come by. Cindy's sisters and cousins, of whom there seemed to be an endless supply, were always at hand. Now the visitors were dwindling, as were the casseroles and phone calls. Cindy said he was scaring people, sitting on the porch all day, day after day, just staring at the house down the street. He was sorry if he was frightening people. He didn't want Cindy's family to stop coming round. It was one of the things he envied about his wife, all these blood ties. Big Bob himself had been an only child and they'd had only had one beloved son. Todd Cameron Yates, aged 19. 1984-2003.

Bob stared down the street and watched the house. He watched the cars pull up and stop. Watched the furtive men and women leave their cars, sometimes with the engines still running, and go into the house for a few minutes, then come out again, get in their Impalas and Beamers and shit-brown Subarus and drive away.

It would be very easy to go into the garage, get the gun and go over there. They would open the door to him, thinking he was just another customer. He wouldn't even have to be a good shot at that range. But he'd promised her. And besides, he felt sure he would get even angrier than he was now. He was not finished brewing.

He went and lay next to her, fitting his long body to the curve of her back without waking her. He didn't want to talk any more. He wanted to wrap his big bulgy arms around Cindy's smooth shoulders, to feel the bones of her ribs beneath the skin. He wanted to breathe in the almond scent of her hair. But he knew that if he embraced her, and if she moved or woke or reached for him, to cry against his chest, that he would shatter into a million pieces. He was afraid, and the fear turned him to something thick and heavy and cold, like a whale washed up on the beach.

After clawing unsuccessfully towards sleep, Bob cautiously got up from the bed and resumed his post in his rocking chair on the porch. He watched the stars and moon and clouds twist with dreadful lethargy across the blue-black sky.

Wednesday afternoon found him still on the porch. He was not ready to go back to work yet. The idea of having to face all those sympathetic customers, asking him for advice on the latest dishwasher or clothes dryer while not asking him what they really wanted to ask, which was, "How could it happen to *your* kid, Bob?" No, he couldn't face that yet, and the store would run perfectly well without him for a while.

He went out to the garage, put the final changes on the sign, and polished the gun even though it already gleamed. There was nothing else to do then, so he went back to sitting. He sat upright and stiff in the big rocker. He pushed back and forth in small, rapid motions, with both big, flat feet firmly on the porch planks. He had worn the same plaid shirt and jeans for he didn't know how many days. Cindy said he was starting to smell, and wanted him to take a shower. But he didn't. He would not eat either, except a hard-boiled egg now and then, and maybe some dry toast. It was all his stomach could keep down. He drank coffee, strong, to keep his mind racing.

Big Bob's mind was edgy and filled with bloody images, which he found comforting even though he understood this was perverse. Images of faces mangled under his fingernails, of hearts on the ends of sticks, of noses cracking under his boot heels. He wallowed in the daydreams, as thick and clingy as tar.

At fifty-two, Big Bob was all muscle and sunburned skin. An outdoorsman. A man with a loud voice he'd never tried to modulate. He prided himself on the amount of space he took up in the world. It was his family's shelter, that space. But he'd been wrong about that, hadn't he? And having been proved wrong, he thought at least he could use his muscle to get some satisfaction.

Last Friday, he had gone back to the police station one last time.

"My name is Bob Yates," he'd said to the pretty, podgy young woman behind a chest-high counter and thick bullet-proof glass. Her hair was in tight braids and her uniform strained across her middle.

"Hello, again, Mr. Yates. How can I help you?" she said.

"I want to talk to someone on the drug squad."

"You'll have to tell me what the problem is first, sir," she said.

He'd raised his voice then. Raised it for a while, until the young woman called someone from behind a door and Bob was passed over to a kid probably not much older than Todd. He had a pimple on his cheek and wore a smile that told Big Bob he hadn't yet seen much action out there on the mean streets. Bob shouldered past any chance of pleasantries.

"I want you to tell me what you people are doing down here," he said in his big-man's voice. "I want you to explain to me why that bunch of scumbag drug dealers is still permitted to operate on my fucking street."

"Mr. Yates, we understand how difficult this time is for you," began the kid.

"No, you don't. So don't give me that shit. I'm not looking for your condescending bull. I want you to get your asses over to 514 Birch Street and I want you to arrest those bastards."

"I assure you, Mr. Yates, a full investigation is underway. The perpetrators will be arrested at the appropriate time. You can understand the department's requirements for proof."

"It's been three fucking weeks. I watch those sons of bitches going about their business like nothing happened and you people don't do a thing about it!"

"Mr. Yates," said the kid, his voice so polite that Big Bob was hard pressed not to break his neck, "we want to stop drug trafficking as much as you do, but you have to understand we're doing everything we can to ensure these criminals get more than just a slap on the wrist. We know what we're doing. We need to get the right people at the right time."

"The right people? I'll give you the right people! Take you over there right now and introduce you. Everybody else sure as hell knows where they live, if you don't. What is it? You waiting for another dead kid?"

"Sir, I understand you're upset . . ."

"You don't understand jack shit, you little twerp."

"Is there a problem here, Constable?" A senior-looking officer came out of a door down the hall. He stood with his hands on his ample hips, puffed out his chest, and made himself into the full measure of a Person-In-Charge.

"No problem. No fucking problem. Except you people don't seem to be able to find your own dicks in a tight pair of BVDs."

He'd stormed out of the station, throwing open the glass door so that it banged against the cement wall.

That was five days ago. He'd known then he was going to have to handle things himself.

He flexed his hands around the blue cup, stared into the cold coffee. He wondered how hard he would have to squeeze before it would pop. He pushed it, testing the limits, wanting to feel the shatter, maybe even see his own blood spilled, but the cup did not break.

Cindy was in the kitchen, on the phone to Valerie, her sister. These days she was either on the phone or lying down. She was manic with the need to talk one minute, then she'd burst into tears and a coma-like sleep would follow. She'd come out to the porch this morning when she got up, swollen-eyed and blotchy, her once-beautiful skin sagged and lined. It seemed she'd aged a decade in the past few weeks. She'd asked him again if he was going to do something stupid. He'd taken her pale hands, held them gently for the bones under his thick fingers were as fragile as those of birds. He'd told her no, he wasn't going to do anything dumb. There was nothing dumb about what he was going to do, he thought. She'd accepted that, probably because it took less energy to do so. He wanted more than anything to put the colour back in her eyes. They looked as though the monsoon of tears had washed out the green, leaving only a pale film behind.

"I miss him, I miss him," she said later into the phone. "I don't understand how we'll live without him." She started to cry again, her hand like a protective wing over her eyes.

Big Bob got up and stretched. He entwined his fingers and pushed out his arms until his knuckles cracked. He rolled his neck and blew out a breath, ran his hand over his scrubbly chin. He walked down the steps and into the garage. The garage was tidy, with a shelf around the walls, up near the ceiling, lined with glass jars of nails, screws, and washers, all sorted by sizes. His tools dangled neatly from aluminium hooks attached to punchboard. Todd's motorcycle, a Norton 750 he'd worked hard for, saved up for, and of which his mother was always afraid, stood next to his own Plymouth. Bob stuck a mallet in the waistband of his pants, picked up the sign and his polished Remington and walked down his driveway and along the street.

There were no cars in front of the brown brick, log-shaped bungalow ten doors along Birch Street. The driveway was cracked and weeds pushed through the asphalt. Plastic bags, an empty yoghurt container and a few empty beer bottles lay scattered in the yard. There was an old tattered sofa on the porch that looked mildewed. A stack of beer cases piled up on the steps. The yard was mostly dirt, just rag-rug scraps of straggly grass. A battered car sat behind the house, next to a tilting garage. The one shutter remaining on the living room window hung from a broken hinge. Bob guessed that maybe the drug business wasn't as lucrative as everyone said it was, or maybe they shot all the proceeds right back into their own veins.

A slouchy and beaten-looking Rottweiler trembled at the end of a chain attached to an empty clothesline. He sniffed the air, trying to get a whiff of Big Bob. There were no other signs of life from inside the house, which was disappointing. Bob stepped onto the lawn. The dog began to growl and its hackles rose. Bob lay the rifle down within easy reach and stuck the end of the sign on the grass. He pulled the mallet out of the top of his pants and began to bang the sign into the ground. As he did so, the dog barked and strained at the end of its chain. Bang! Bang! Bang! The earth was soft and yielding and the sign slipped in easily. Big Bob had written the same thing on both sides so the inhabitants of the house would be sure to see it.

DRUGS SOLD HERE!
GET YOUR CRACK HERE!

Big Bob picked up the rifle and waited. The dog barked, foam flying from its muzzle, its eyes rolling and its ears flat. The door opened, and a man peered out.

"What the fuck is going on out here?" He was whippet-thin, with long dark hair and a droopy moustache blending into unshaven, sunken cheeks. He wore a Toronto Blue Jays baseball cap, black jeans with holes at the knees and a white T-shirt with the words "Muff Diver" written above a cartoon of an evil-looking hillbilly – to whom he bore some resemblance – preparing to leap between the legs of a buxom young gal. The man scanned the scene in front of him, apparently not able to focus properly this early in the day. Then he registered Big Bob and the gun and the sign.

He reached around to the back of his pants and Bob assumed he was reaching for a handgun. Bob levelled the rifle at him, hoping, praying the guy would give him an excuse to fire it.

"I don't know who you are, mister, but I'm telling you to get the fuck off my lawn and take this shit with you."

"I'm the Un-welcome Wagon. Here to tell you to get your crap loaded up and haul ass out of my neighbourhood," said Big Bob.

"Get the fuck outta here, you crazy asshole!"

"I'm going to be here every day, bud. You take this sign down, I'm going to be here in an hour to put another one in its place. Seems the police were having a little trouble finding you, so I'm here to make sure they can't miss you."

The man stepped out onto the stoop and was just about to say something when a wraith-like girl wearing only a tattered oversized T-shirt appeared in the doorway.

"Jimmy, don't!" she said, and clawed his arm.

"Get back in the house, Dinah!" he yelled, and pushed her. She wore nothing under the filthy T-shirt and Bob was ashamed that, as she stumbled and hit the door, he could see her shrivelled thighs, her hairy sex.

"Ignore him, just ignore him, he'll go away," said the girl called Dinah. She looked at him, pulling the T-shirt down. "Please, mister, just go away, go away!"

"The smartest thing you could do right now is listen to the lady, pal," said the skinny man, his right hand still behind his back.

Bob saw another movement in the doorway. A child, maybe three years old, came and stood near the woman, who made no effort to move her to safety. The little girl had a tangled mess of brown, greasy hair and a scab on her left knee. Her legs were so thin they looked like grey twigs. She sucked her thumb. She wore only a pair of dingy underpants and there was a bruise on her arm.

Bob wanted very badly to shoot the man. He knew he would probably be doing the little girl a favour. What kind of a father could this human pustule be? What chance did she have? She'd be better off an orphan. It would be over so quickly. The man was saying something, but Bob wasn't paying attention. He could see his lips moving, but he could make out no sound. In his mind he was bringing the gun up to his shoulder and taking aim, he was pulling the friendly little trigger and the man's chest was blossoming out in a pretty red flower. It would feel indescribably good to shoot him and see him clutch at his heart and writhe on the ground the way Todd did, night after night, in Bob's nightmares. Maybe the man would also shoot him. He wondered if he'd mind very much. He was unable to decide.

"Bob! Bob! Oh, God, somebody call the police! Bob!" Cindy's panicked cries reached him, and although he didn't want to take his eyes off the man's hand, he assumed Cindy was running down the street. He'd have to decide what he was going to do rather quickly.

The little girl pulled her thumb out of her mouth and her forehead puckered. Then, having drawn some private conclusion about this new man standing on her lawn, she laughed. Tiny little pearls of baby teeth in a soft pink mouth. She stood there, smiling as though Bob were her favourite uncle. No one was more surprised than Bob when he smiled back.

He supposed he wasn't going to be able to shoot anyone today. Big Bob lowered the rifle, turned, and walked away. His legs felt as though they were made of unravelling twine.

Cindy ran down the street toward him, her feet in house slippers, her hair undone, her mouth open wide, but no sound came out. Her hands were outstretched as though she ran from something burning. He sat down in the middle of the street and looked around. The doors of his neighbours' houses were open and people were coming toward him, others peeked out from behind the safety of half-drawn curtains. One man stood at the end of his driveway and applauded.

Bob put the gun down on the street next to him and held his arms out to his wife. Cindy threw herself down on the dusty asphalt next to him, crying and patting him all over to make sure he was whole and not bleeding. Bob took her hands – her pale, fragile, trembling hands – between his palms and put them, like a common prayer, up to his face.

# WINGS

Lily caught her heel in a sidewalk grate and imagined a hand reaching through the steel grid. She distrusted grates and long suspected such a thing might be possible. Then, seeing her foot so trapped, she blushed and struggled to free herself. When she had been a Pretty Young Thing such a predicament would have produced, in no time at all, some strapping young man, eager to ease her from her snare. Now, however, she was invisible and afraid of falling. She slipped her square toes from their sheath and balanced on one foot, teetering and awkward, while she pulled roughly on the shoe. The metal scraped the leather, twisted the heel, and dislodged the little plastic end. Lily's lip trembled, which made her blush all the more, but it was such a lovely shoe. Walking on it like that would ruin it. She put it back on and limped to a nearby shoe repair store.

"Excuse me," she said to the little man behind the counter, "my shoe, can you fix it?" The cobbler, a stubby little man, turned and blinked, as though surprised to see anyone. In his hand, he held a short, pungent cigar. He took the shoe from her with a grunt.

"Take time. Come back three days."

"I can't do that. I have no other shoe." She smiled. "I am at your mercy."

"Huh," said the man. "Huh. Wait." He turned away.

She was going to miss her train back to the suburbs, but it couldn't be helped. While she waited, Lily drew her tweed coat around her middle and held her brown purse, her good purse, which she had taken out of the plastic bag in the back of the closet especially for this occasion. She did not take going to an afternoon concert, her first matinee ever, lightly. Bach. It had been lovely. She stood pressed to the window in the shoemaker's tiny store, which smelled of the acrid cigar, of rubber, feet, dust, and burnt metal from the harsh machine for grinding keys. She watched the people passing, the businessmen bent forward with strict intent, the young mothers bustling babies along in carriages, the slouching teenagers in their baggy, ill-fitting clothes.

It was then that she saw the strange, almost cloud-like shape. *What on earth? What am I seeing?* It could not be what it looked like . . . and yet it was. A young man. It was a young man with white wings. A young man with white wings walking nonchalantly down the sunny side of the street.

Lily watched the young man. He was not abnormally tall, but the way the waves of people parted, it seemed as though he was. The young man wore white overalls, the kind that painters wear, with dome snaps up the front. He wore black boots, with heavy soles. And on his back curved large white wings covering the space from head to knees. They were very beautiful wings, heavy and gleaming white, but no one paid the slightest notice. Just as though he was, like her, an invisible old woman.

Lily was struck by an impulse to run after him. However, hobbled as she was with one shoe on and one shoe off, she certainly couldn't leave the shop to follow a man who had white wings. She craned her neck, not wanting to lose sight of him. He went into a coffee shop and came out a moment later, carrying a paper cup. He stood, sipping whatever drink was inside. The way people ignored him puzzled Lily, for she could see no reason he should share her affliction of invisibility. He was neither old, nor was he nondescript. A man with white wings could be called many things, but unremarkable was not one of them. And although she could not see his eyes, she felt sure they would be interesting, arresting eyes. Very pale blue perhaps, or very dark brown. His hair was black, and long, but not so long as to be unkempt. Even here, in the city, where people were accustomed to all sorts of strange sights, wouldn't this at least merit a second glance?

Lily's own grey hair nestled in a soft knot at her neck. In her ears, she wore rather large and well-cut diamond studs. They had been a gift from her husband (she still thought of him that way, no matter what), on their twenty-fifth wedding anniversary. They were the very same earrings she had vowed to flush down the toilet when, on their twenty-sixth anniversary, he had announced he was leaving her for Mary Donnell.

"You know, *Mary*," Douglas had said, "Mary in *Accounting*." As though she did. As though that would explain anything.

In the end, in the post-storm quiet of her empty house, she had not been able bring herself to flush away the sparkling evidence of what a liar he was, although for many years neither had she worn them. She had only taken them up again in an attempt to hold the fog of disappearing at bay. Perhaps if people no longer saw her, they might see the flash of lost love's metaphor on her ears.

Sometimes it worked, but as often, it failed, and she sat in restaurants, the last to be served. She sat at church socials, against a pale yellow cinder-block wall with a thin cup of tea and watched families drift past, families who never stopped to chat. She sat on park benches, where only the pigeons paid her any mind, and then, she suspected, only because of the bread she offered. She sat in buses, where gangs of young people jostled her and never offered a seat.

No one jostled the beautiful young man with white wings, but neither did they purposefully step aside. It seemed they simply did not notice him, for if they had, Lily was sure they would turn and at the very least smile, for she knew that people were made glad by beauty.

Men used to smile at her. She tried to remember when that had changed.

*Ah yes.* She had been in her late thirties, walking past a construction site. A whistle, and what could only be referred to as a hoot, had cut through the sound of traffic. Lily had looked to see what poor girl was the recipient of such loathsome male posturing but she was the only woman on the block. Three men in hard hats, overalls and heavy boots leaned over a concrete wall. One ate a sandwich wrapped in wax paper. They waved at her and one said, "Oooooh, baby, looking *good* today. Looking *good!*" For a moment she had been stunned. Then she'd laughed, which seemed to confuse the men, and they looked nervously at one another, fearful perhaps, that they had whistled at a lunatic. But Lily wasn't crazy. She'd laughed because it had been months and months, and in fact she couldn't remember when, since she'd walked past a construction site and someone had whistled at her.

"Thanks, boys," she'd said. "At my age, believe me, it's a compliment!"

The men had guffawed in a relieved sort of way then and one of them had tipped his hard hat.

"If you're going to be here tomorrow, I'll come back," she'd said.

"It'd be a pleasure, ma'am, a real pleasure."

And she'd smiled and blushed and tried not to think about the "ma'am."

So when had being noticed by men become so rare it took her off guard? And why had it suddenly felt not like an insult, or even a compliment, but like a kindness? Perhaps she should have felt a newly found liberation, but instead she felt as though she'd had something surgically removed. Something she would miss very much.

At first, Lily had thought the encroaching foggy "no-where-ness" was the result of diminishing beauty, for she'd once had the easy assurance that came from knowing you are pleasing people simply by providing them with something appealing to look at. But all beauty fades, until you are just a blur against the wall.

She had counted on a vibrant, interesting personality and a keen mind to keep her visible in the world, until her mother, Thelma, then seventy-one, divested her of this delusion. Thelma had never been pretty. She was a raw-boned athletic woman, with a hawk nose and a fleshy, masculine mouth. But she was brilliant; a doctor in an age when few women had aspired to a career outside the home, which Lily assumed had given her mother consolation for her somewhat unappealing face and form.

Physically, age had not been any kinder to Thelma than youth had been, but Lily had been inspired by the way her mother apparently discounted the tyranny of beauty, and held the older woman as a role model. It had shocked her, then, that day in her mother's bedroom, watching her lean into the mirror. The older woman had lifted her liver-spotted hands to either side of her face and pushed backwards. The effect had been clownish.

"I don't recognize myself some days," Thelma had said. "Inside I still feel like a girl of twenty-five, but look, look at that face." She had taken her hands away and the folds and dewlaps fell back. "Whose face *is* that?"

"You've never complained about your face before," Lily had said, and the words were out of her mouth before she'd had time to consider the benefits of silence.

"Do you know what Dr. Billings said to me when I went to see him last week for my check-up?"

Lily had sighed. Her mother had at least six check-ups a year and was in perfect health, contrary to her assertions that she was on the brink of a major cardiovascular "event."

"No, what did Dr. Billings say?"

"He said I was so very nice and clean." Thelma had huffed disgustedly at her own reflection. "*Clean* for heaven's sake. And that's the best compliment I've had in years. That I'm clean. God, it's enough to make a woman take herself off to the cliffs. But you'll see." Lily's breath had caught at the barely contained anger in the older woman's voice. "It'll happen to you. You get old. People don't see you anymore."

Lily later concluded what she'd suspected all along: men did not suffer the same fate as women. Douglas had not become invisible. Her husband had become the proud father of a newborn when he was sixty-two. Perhaps the secret was children, perhaps she should have had a child, but there was nothing she could do about that now. For men so many things were different. And so Lily tried to accept that the invisibility of ageing was, like so many other injustices, primarily the domain of women.

Which did nothing to explain the young man with beautiful white wings.

Seen from this distance, she could almost believe they were made of real feathers. They were cannily formed, silk perhaps, with each feather delicately overlapping and ruffling in the spring breeze. She wondered if he were in a play. The young man walked with a jaunty step and as he did his wings bobbed and bounced in a happy way.

She had not considered the possibility of wings. Wings would make a person feel special even if, as it now seemed, they did little to command attention. They would be regal and beautiful, no matter what dreadful husk huddled below.

"Hey," the cobbler said, "you shoe. You shoe is fix." He blew cigar smoke in her direction and she wondered if it provided a more solid outline for her dwindling self, like smoke in front of a motion detector beam. He dangled her shoe at the end of his finger, as though an old woman's shoe was unsanitary.

She paid him and hurried into the street, straining to see the young man with white wings. He waited patiently at the corner for a red light to change. People stood all around, but no one paid him the least bit of attention. Not even a little boy, playing "walk the dog" with a yo-yo in one hand and holding his mother's hand with the other. Lily walked as rapidly as her old knees would allow.

The young man stepped into the intersection. An African man, dressed in a magnificent robe splashed with all the colours of autumn, walked near him and as he did, he turned his head for a fraction of a second, then hopped two steps to make up, perhaps, for lost time. He shook his head, and seemed to chuckle. Lily moved quickly. She wanted to ask where she could get wings like those. Surely if she had soft white wings, she wouldn't mind disappearing. She would be safe beneath their gentle arc, their sweet protective shade. She was right behind him. She stepped into the busy street, and reached out to the warm, hopeful promise of feathers.

# AN UNREHEARSED DESIRE

Charlotte and Amy meet for lunch at the new Cuban restaurant on John Street. They take a table in the corner, away from the draughty front door. The air smells of frying onions and peppers. They sit under palm fronds and a lazy ceiling fan, while outside the cold wind blows up from frozen Lake Ontario. They eat rice with pork and corn, fragrant with garlic, annato oil and coloured a deep gold with *bijol*. They sip beer and try to pretend it's a stormy day in Havana.

Amy, dressed in scarves and boots and flouncing gypsy skirts, like an upscale rendition of Stevie Nicks, tells Charlotte about the weekend she and her husband, Dan, spent at the Millwood Inn. Romantic, Amy says, and blushes a little, which annoys Charlotte who thinks it falsely coy.

"Lucky you," says Charlotte, looking past Amy to the burnished mirror and her own blond, sleek-haired reflection. She presses the tip of her baby finger to the corner of her mouth, erasing an errant smudge of red lipstick. "Although a weekend in the country with nothing to do except Arnie is my idea of hell."

Amy arranges her face into an expression Charlotte recognizes: it's the one intended to encourage confidence.

Charlotte thinks how pouched Amy's under-eyes look. *She tries to look so young. It's pathetic.* Contempt is easy, yet she cannot deny it is the mirror-twin of envy. When was the last time she had had a romantic weekend, or wanted one?

"Is everything all right between you and Arnie?" Amy says, leaning forward, elbows on the table, hands clasped.

"As right as it's ever been."

"Which means?"

"It means Arnie's a good man, a good father, a good husband."

"And?"

"And, simply put, he revolts me." There it is. Charlotte knows she has shocked Amy and she wants to shock her more. "Sex, from what I remember, is an exercise in gritting my teeth."

"Well, it's only temporary, surely. What do you expect, Charlotte?" she says, her eyes wide enough to suggest she might have a thyroid condition. "You've been married for twenty-six years. Things change."

"No, they don't. That's just the problem. They just stay the same. Only more so."

Charlotte drains her beer and orders another from a beautiful young man with gold-flecked brown eyes. She changes the subject, and Amy looks relieved.

Later, Charlotte sits in her car in the parking lot and rests her forehead on the steering wheel. She thinks about just driving, like people do in the movies. The credits roll while the heroine sets off to a new life and a soulful voice sings about any place being better than this.

She raises her head and sees the attendant looking at her from his little booth. He probably thinks she's drunk. She isn't, but she wishes she were. She starts the ignition. She has to pick up the dry cleaning on the way home.

All the way along the 401 she hears the sound of her own voice telling Amy how her husband disgusts her. Surprising, how awful it sounded, put into words that way. But there it was. The truth of it. She has never found Arnie beautiful, never thrilled to the sight of his flesh, never wanted to run her tongue along any part of his anatomy, and over the years, this ambivalence has deepened to loathing. She fooled herself, in the early days, into thinking it hadn't really mattered.

It was, after all, his bookishness that had attracted her to Arnie in the first place. She overlooked his narrow shoulders in favour of his keen mind. If his kisses were too wet, his hands too tentative and his genitals so remarkably unremarkable, at least he was witty and sharp and could recite Neruda and Whitman.

But *Leaves of Grass* has been forever replaced with stock quotes and investment portfolios. The quiet house that neither hides nor muffles her hollow footsteps has replaced the safety margin of children and familial life. The children are grown and gone and there isn't even an echo of the passionate, if once-removed, rhythms that poetry offered.


It is nearly dinnertime now and Charlotte pats at the chilly flesh of tonight's chicken with a paper towel. It sticks to the bumpy skin, like toilet paper to the shaving nick on Arnie's neck when he came down for breakfast this morning. Charlotte sprinkles salt and pepper into the gaping, faintly embarrassing cavity and daydreams about a boy she knew in school when she was eighteen. His name was David and all the parents knew him as *That Boy*. A bad boy in that good way that makes young girls blush and giggle behind their nibble-nailed hands. His sandy hair hung down on his forehead like Marlon Brando and his eyes squinted like James Dean. Oh, how his chinos hung on his hips, which were slim as arrows and just as deadly. He sat in the cafeteria, tilted back on the two legs of a rickety chair, his knees wide apart. If only she'd known then what she knows now. She would have knelt between those thighs and done things that back then only bad girls did. Fifty-seven-year-old Charlotte pushes her gold-rimmed glasses up the bridge of her nose and thinks she should have been a bad girl.

That night in bed, Arnie reaches for her and she permits it, out of guilt for the daydreams and the lunch-talk betrayal. He puts his hand on her hip as he lies next to her in his cotton pyjamas. She thinks of his hand with the long fingers and blue-green veins swelling the surface of the thin skin. She wills herself not to push it away, not to speak. The hand moves in gentle circles, polishes her hip through the fabric of her flannel nightgown.

"I love you," Arnie whispers in her ear, his breath warm and smelling of peppermint toothpaste.

"Love you, too." Her voice is too high-pitched to ring true.

The hand squeezes her hip in a knowing way, a resigned way, and Arnie settles into sleep around her. Charlotte's jaw relaxes. Another bedtime successfully navigated.


Thursday. She has an appointment to get her teeth cleaned. The dentist says her gums are receding from years of brushing too hard. He tells her they will have to operate, taking skin from the roof of her mouth and grafting it to her tooth-tops. Not uncommon in someone her age, he says, and Charlotte walks out on the verge of tears.

She finds herself in mid-day lunchtime chaos in Yorkville. Pert young things are everywhere, mobile phones held to their ears like industrial jewellery. She walks along the avenue, her collar turned against the wind. She feels as though she must treat herself to something. Celebrate something in the face of nothing at all to celebrate.

She'd like to go into a café, sit and drink espresso from a tiny cup. She'd like to have a talk with someone at another table, a perfect stranger who read Kafka or who had paint spatters on his hands. She looks in the windows of a store selling hats. Perhaps she should buy a hat, something that would sit on her head like a billboard – shouting out who she really was. A remarkable hat that would be a statement of her artsy side, for she is sure she has one. But she'd look ridiculous, surely, like she was trying too hard.

Perhaps a glass of wine, then. And a plate of olives and cheese. She looks into a restaurant window. A girl in a daffodil-yellow mini-dress sits at a tiny table. She has her arms flung around the shoulders of two young men, one as dark as the other is pale. She throws her head back and laughs at something, and as she does the pale one stares down at her breasts while the dark one glares at his rival. All Charlotte can think is how cold the girl must be.

She can't go in there.

But what can she do?

Charlotte thinks she very well might cry.

She scans the street and her eyes settle on a sign. It's a large pair of bright red neon lips, above the words *Lovefest – the lover's paradise.* She walks over. The window displays a variety of rubber and leather items: boots, corsets, panties and masks. There are candles and bottles of oils. There are massage manuals. The door opens and a red-haired woman in her thirties, dressed in a chic grey cashmere coat, steps out. She smiles at Charlotte and holds the door open for her.

*What the hell,* thinks Charlotte. She says thank you and steps inside. The first thing she sees is an alcove containing a four-foot-high penis, carved out of ivory. Charlotte giggles and then immediately stops herself. She does not want to look like a silly blushing teenager. She has a right to be here. She has nothing of which to be ashamed. She walks over to look at the giant penis and reads the card on the wall, which explains that it is a seventh-century Japanese phallic symbol, used as an altar item in a fertility cult. *Well, fancy that!*

Charlotte steps deeper into the shop and is amazed at how large, well-lit and busy it is. There is one main room and two more leading off on either side of the sales counter.

There is a lingerie section, a book section, a leather and rubber section, shelves of oils and perfumes and edible panties.
There is a long glass counter containing what looks like an
assortment of personal vibrators and penises. There is a blow-
up doll leaning against a wall, tastefully attired in a short
black cocktail dress. The store isn't crowded certainly, but
more people than she'd anticipated – well-dressed people of
all ages – mill about with little red baskets slung over their
arms, picking out their purchases.

Charlotte suppresses a grin and feels a flush that is decid-
edly not menopausal. She is being very naughty, and she
likes it. She is being an adventuress. On a small table next to
her is a bowl of tiny chocolate penises and breasts, with a
sign saying "Help Yourself" in a friendly script. She does. The
small penis melts warmly and smoothly in her mouth. She
feels comfort and pleasure. It occurs to her that she has not
come into this store by chance, but that she has been led
here, to this portal into another world, a world she had never
known. Her fingertips tingle with anticipation of the sensual
possibilities all around her.

She passes a rack of French maid outfits: bustiers and little white aprons and caps and tiny panties with just a string
up the back. No, she thinks, imagining discomfort, that's not
for me. It dawns on her that she is looking for something
here that will please her, something that will stir up the caul-
dron of her desires. She feels both furtive and bold, and her
left hand goes to her face, the index and middle finger placed
lightly on the side of her mouth, as though she were a
woman in a market, picking through cabbages and radishes.

She looks at a shelf of books. One has a picture of a young girl bent over a bed. She wears black stockings and high heels, but nothing else. Her passive face is turned towards the camera and her bottom is raised high in the air. Charlotte blushes, but not unpleasantly. Next to the rack of books is a selection of paddles and riding crops. Charlotte's pulse is palpable in her neck. She is aroused just looking at these items, and imagines warmth on her buttocks, as though the paddle had been applied.

Next, she looks in the glass case. In it are a series of rubber penises, some of a most extraordinary size. They are in an assortment of colours: red, black, white, and even green, a colour that instantly produces a rather strange set of fantasies involving aliens. Some of the penises have straps attached. One or two look astonishingly real, although surely not to scale. Surely not. Some seem to come with batteries.

"May I help you?" asks a smiling, pretty, young woman with very white teeth. "Would you like me to show you one of these?" she says.

"I don't think so, thank you," Charlotte blushes again, but now it is anything but comfortable. "I'm just looking."

"No problem. Let me know if you need any help." The girl moves away.

It enters Charlotte's mind that she could have one of these, if she wished. She could simply point and say *Yes, I'd like that 15-inch red model, with the circumcised head.* She could pay for it, and that would be that, she would take it home and use it, when no one was around, when she was alone on her king-sized bed, lolling naked in the afternoon sun.

But no, she wouldn't do that. She couldn't. But, oh, how she craves and longs for something, some little thing, some object that would be a symbol of her sexuality.

She turns and sees a rack of small items. A stick with ostrich plumes on the end (perhaps hope is a thing with feathers after all, she thinks), pots of love-gel in various flavours, rings to put in piercings on various parts of the body, from earlobes to labia. Her eyes fix on a series of small clamps, some with jewels dangling from them, some with tassels. A discreet card identifies them: *Nipple Clamps*.

Charlotte's mouth opens and closes, twice. She is immediately aware of her breasts, the weight of them inside her bra. She can almost feel the tiny clamps around her nipples, painful, but not too painful, pulling and jiggling. Her breath comes in short puffs. Images involving the bottom of the girl at the bed, the paddle, the clamps, and a faceless man with no mercy in his eyes, fill her mind. Her panties are damper than they have been since she entered menopause.

Charlotte must have those clamps, the ones with the little green jewels dangling from the ends like envious tears. She has to have them. It occurs to her that the packages are very small. Hardly any noticeable size at all. She could simply slip one into her pocket, and who would notice?

She looks into the gilt-framed mirror above the case and scans the room to see if anyone is watching. It seems to Charlotte that the room has become very still, that her beating heart is the epicentre of all the activity, and by its heavy thudding, it has taken all the movement from elsewhere and stilled it. Her hand reaches out and slides the nipple clamps, in their hygienic plastic packet, into her roomy and accommodating pocket.

With her treasure safe, the room begins to move again. Charlotte's heart pounds and a slight sheen appears on her upper lip. She fans her coat open as though she were having a hot flash, which she decides is a stroke of genius. No one could possibly suspect her of anything, not a menopausal homemaker in a camel-hair coat.

She spends a few minutes wandering about, looking at this and that. There is no hurry. Hurry would be a mistake. Hurry would indicate something was amiss. She must be nonchalant. She putters about, looking at a series of prints from the *Kama Sutra*. Then she decides it is enough, that she must go now, go home and try on her treasures.

Calmly she walks to the door, nodding politely at the salesgirl with the white teeth. As she passes the great ivory phallic symbol, a loud beeping noise startles her, her throat closes and she blinks several times, quickly. She feels a hand on her arm and she jumps.

"Oh, isn't it silly? Probably just a tag on something you have," says the pretty girl. "Would you come with me, please? We'll find the culprit."

"What is this about?" says Charlotte.

The girl's hand tightens slightly. She smiles reassuringly at a gaggle of shoppers who have turned to stare. "Sybil, can you handle the cash please? Back in a tick." As the girl ushers her to the rear of the store Charlotte catches a glimpse of a surly-looking woman, dressed head to foot in black, behind the cash. The woman looks at her with a smug smile on her heavy face and Charlotte's stomach flips over.

At the rear of the store Charlotte is gently but firmly urged into a small back office.

"I think I may be sick."

"That's too bad," says the girl. "Why not sit down." Charlotte sits on a hard metal chair. "Now, I'm afraid I have to ask you to open your purse and empty your pockets. Store policy. No exceptions, I'm afraid." The girl sounds too chipper, too perky to be sincere. She rhymes off these instructions as though it were the spiel at a burger joint. When Charlotte's face pales, she adds, "Don't worry, goes off all the time, probably just a tag on something from another store." Charlotte has no parcels. "You did buy something somewhere else, right?"

"I don't have anything." Charlotte clutches her purse tightly in her lap. Her lower lip begins to tremble. "I think I should just go home."

"Jeez," the girl giggles a little. "Wish it were that simple, but Sybil saw you put something in your pocket. I said she must have made a mistake, but she said she was sure, and hey, the detector doesn't lie." The girl giggles again.

If the girl had not laughed at her, if she had been cold and officious, Charlotte believes she would have been able to talk her way into some sort of a dignified compromise. But being laughed at by a little blonde with a twenty-three-inch waist and blue fingernail polish is too much. Charlotte begins to cry. Her nose runs. She doesn't want to reach in her pocket for a tissue because she's afraid to pull out her treasure.

"I think you better show me."

"I want to go home! Can't you just let me go home?"

"No. It's store policy. Would you show me what's in your pocket, please?" The girl looks down at the floor and puts her hand out, as though Charlotte were an errant child. She has no choice. She reaches into her pocket, removes her tawdry jewels and puts them in the girl's smooth palm.

"Oh, for God's sake. Why didn't you just buy 'em? They don't cost but 20 bucks!"

"I couldn't. Don't you understand? I just couldn't." Charlotte begins to cry harder and gets the hiccups. "What are – hic – you going to – hic – do with me?"

"Lady, I don't have a choice. I gotta call the cops."

The shock cures her hiccups. Police? Yes, of course there would be police. Arnie would have to know. *Oh, God. Arnie!* She looks at the girl, panic-stricken. Then her stomach rolls and she knows she is going to throw up. The girl knows it too.

"Oh, jeez," she says, and grabs a garbage pail.

When she has finished, the girl says, "Don't move." She picks up the pail with the ends of her fingers and disappears from the room, only to return a moment later with a glass of water and a box of tissues. "Here."

Charlotte trembles from head to foot, so hard that water sloshes over the top of the glass, marking her skirt. She manages a sip and swipes at her mouth, but she can't stop crying and she can't catch her breath and she wants to say something, but she can't think of what and even if she knew, she wouldn't be able to get enough air in her lungs.

"Hey, lady, take it easy. It's not the end of the world."

Oh, but it is. It is surely the end of Charlotte's world. She will go to jail. She will be booked, like Hugh Grant. She will go to court and be on probation, that at least, but surely they wouldn't send her to jail for this, not for this? There is a strange sound coming from her mouth, a thin and ragged wail, a small sound on the outside, but inside her head it sounds like a hurricane-force shriek.

"It's okay. Really, it's going to be okay." The girl pats her on the shoulder and bends down. "You know, you remind me of my mum," she says, which loosens the lump in Charlotte's throat and permits the keening to begin in earnest. "Oh, jeez, oh shit, stay here," says the girl and leaves the room.

Charlotte knows she has gone to call the police. They will be here any minute and she will go to jail in handcuffs. She will be taken out of this store in handcuffs and people will see her on the street, in the back of the police car. Like a prostitute. A prostitute with nipple clamps.

She tries very hard to give herself a heart attack. Or perhaps a stroke. Yes. A stroke would be best. She presses her thumbs into her temples hard enough to make her whimper through the tears.

The door opens and the girl is back, with a mobile phone in her hand.

"Look, I spoke to the manager, okay. I wouldn't even have done that but Sybil saw you, you know, and she'd tell Monica for sure and then *I'd* be in trouble. So, I called her and told her about you and how upset you are and everything. I mean, jeez, it's only 20 bucks, and she said if you buy it it'll be okay and you can go but just don't come back. So, it's okay now, really. You can stop crying. Please stop crying."

And even if it will be okay, if being banned from a store that sells sexual aids is okay, and being a shoplifter is okay, it is still *not okay* and Charlotte can't stop crying because she thought she would be a different person with her treasure, a woman with more passion, and now she is less, not more, and she is coming apart at the thought of having to walk out of this store and find a cab and get home. She can't do that. She can't get up and walk through the store with those people looking at her, knowing that she is exactly what they think she is. The room spins.

"Listen, do you want me to call someone?" says the girl.

"Please, call my husband. Make Arnie come and get me!" The words are out of her mouth before she knew she was going to say them.

She hands the girl her purse, because she might as well look inside, she has nothing more to hide. "His number at the office is in my address book. It's under our name."

The girl smiles at her and says, "You'll have to tell me your name."

Charlotte does and the girl says she'll get her a cup of tea and she does and then goes out to call Arnie because Charlotte can't talk. She stares, crying, at the closed door, and doesn't drink the tea because she's afraid she'll be sick again, and by the time she hears Arnie's voice in the shop it's cold.

"What is the item in question?" says Arnie.

"It wasn't anything much. Just these, eh?"

"I see." There is a pause. "I believe this will cover it. May I take my wife home now?"

"Sure. She's in there. I hope she's okay. She seems like a nice lady."

"You've been very understanding. I'll take it from here," says Arnie, and the chill in his voice in turn chills Charlotte. Her tears stop and she stands as he opens the door and gestures for her to follow him.

They get in the car, she on her side, and he on his. He does not open the door for her, nor indicate in any other way that he is concerned for her. Charlotte knows he must be furious and mortified. She is beyond mortification, in an icy corner of hell, saved for the stupendously stupid. Charlotte turns toward him and opens her mouth to apologize, perhaps, or lie and say it was all a mistake.

"Not a word, Charlotte," he says, holding up a hand turned with its palm toward her, while keeping his eyes in front of him. "I do not want you to speak. Not one single word." His voice is very low and even. It is a very controlled voice.

And so they do not speak on the drive home. Arnie drives the car and Charlotte sits looking out the window. She hopes she will never have to speak again. She will go home and go up to bed. She will pull the covers over her head and stay there until she dies of hunger or shame, whichever comes first.

Arnie pulls the car into the garage and turns off the engine. They go into the house, which seems both too big and too small at the same time. As he takes her coat from her, he speaks and asks if she's all right. She says that no, she is not. She tells him she is sorry. Very sorry. She doesn't know what came over her. She says she is going to bed and walks toward the stairs.

"Charlotte, come here," he calls from the living room. She stops on the lowest stair, but doesn't turn around. She is sure that he will start yelling at her and if he does, she will fall irrevocably apart.

"I said come here, *now* please."

What choice has she? She deserves whatever she gets. Let him say what he wants. Get it over with. She walks into the living room. Arnie stands leaning against the mantle. He looks slim and cruelly elegant in his dark suit, flawlessly un-ruffled even now. In his right hand, he dangles the nipple clamps.

"Charlotte, sit down on the couch."

She sits and waits while he regards her.

"Now, take off your blouse."

Charlotte's eyes leap to his face.

"I mean it," he says. "Do it." He jiggles the clamps slightly so that the green jewels dance.

Oh my, she thinks. Oh my. Charlotte undoes her buttons, one by one, as her breathing quickens.

# FOR MARLENE,
# WHO BECAME A BEAR

## WHEN IT STARTED, ROUGHLY

People considered Marlene strange even as a child, long before she took to living as a bear on society's hinterland. Special. Fragile. Quirky. Any one of the adjectives used in the nicer circles of society, into which Marlene had been born in 1940, to describe someone such as her.

In fact, she came from good solid stock, and if the source of her later maladjustment couldn't be found there, the seeds of her indisputable brilliance could. Marlene's mother, Daphne Hatterson (née Fitzwilliams of the Boston Fitzwilliams), was a columnist for the *Philadelphia Herald* who wrote under the well-known, if somewhat transparent *nom de plume,* Fitzwilly. Her father was the celebrated legal mind Daniel Hatterson, a man who never gave up on a case, no matter how bleak his prospects at winning.

Marlene inherited her parents' intelligence, so although she was certainly an odd duck, she was never a dim one. She was smart as a whip, a phrase her mother often used to deflect criticism from her unusual child. But what did *that* mean? Marlene wondered, since it was the whip's victim who felt the smartness, the serpent of leather itself being but a droopy thing, and not smart at all. It was effect, in other words, not a state of being. These sorts of questions perplexed Marlene, and she voiced her queries quite loudly to anyone who would listen, much to the chagrin of her parents, who only smiled gently to puzzled guests as though they found their daughter amusing and not exasperating.

Marlene insisted on calling her mother, not Mum, not Ma, not Mother, not even Mommy (which would have been bad enough) but Daph. "What if," she asked when she was a girl of twelve, "what if, Daph, you could take the Bible, well, the Old Testament, in the original Aramaic or Hebrew, of course, transpose the letters to their numerological correspondents, then transpose the numbers to associated musical notes and create chords from the words?"

"What?" said Daphne. She was preoccupied at the keyboard of her Underwood, as she often was. In this instance she was trying to find the right word, with a flavour both bitter and bold, condescending and protesting, to describe her outrage at the antics of that idiot drunk, Joe McCarthy. Senator McCarthy. It was 1952 ,for God's sake, not the witch trials of Salem, and Daphne had made it her rather perilous business to champion the cause of the Hollywood Ten, only partly because she thought Humphrey Bogart the most attractive of men.

"Daph, you're not listening! I mean, it's possible, isn't it, and what would it sound like? Do you think it would be the sound of Yahweh, the noise of creation, music of the spheres, in the flesh, so to speak, or sing, or whatever . . ." the words came out in a rush and some of them surprised Marlene, unaware as she was that they had been inside her.

"Good God!" Daphne blinked. "Is this what you spend your time doing? You think too much. Isn't there a tree you want to climb or something?"

Daphne had never understood even the most ordinary of children very well and would not have had any, had dear Daniel not insisted. Inwardly, she cursed because she felt the skein of her thought unravelling in front of her. *Yahweh? What on earth was the girl talking about?*

"But really, it's possible, isn't it? Daph! Think of all the implications! Celestial resonance!" Marlene shifted her weight from one foot to the other, rambling about the prospects, the limitless prospects of such a theory. She held her chubby arms tight at her sides, and clasped her hands, still dimpled with baby fat, under her chin as though in prayer.

"Celestial resonance? Where do you get these words?"

Precocious was one thing, but Daphne worried about Marlene. The way she spoke sometimes sounded, almost, well, crazy. "She's a brilliant girl – just slightly high strung," said Mrs. Wallbridge, Marlene's teacher, at parent-teacher night. "You simply must stimulate her mind." Daphne, however, suspected that might be the very problem – far too much stimulation. The girl never seemed to relax, to play like other children. Her constant excitement and her never-ending revelations were exhausting. Not to mention that she hated being called Daph, a diminutive she feared might not refer to her name as a term of affection, but rather to Daffy Duck, a cartoon character Marlene could imitate perfectly and had once called the Antichrist.

"Thrummed by the Heavens, Daph! We'd be out of control!" Marlene turned in circles, round and round the room, which Daphne so optimistically called her study.

"Simmer down, Marlene. Calm yourself." She stared over the top of her cat's-eye glasses at the flushed girl and wished for the thousandth time that her husband would spend less time at the office and more time helping her raise the child he had so desperately wanted. Tragically, however, Daniel Hatterson would soon be spending no time at all with his daughter, or with anyone else for that matter.

Marlene's father died suddenly and somewhat dramatically. The respected orator expired, one Thursday afternoon, of a stroke that felled him in the middle of a particularly impassioned plea for the jury to find his client innocent. The degree of fervour with which Daniel Hatterson cajoled, entreated, bullied and exhorted his case was necessitated by the fact that his client was so obviously guilty of the gruesome crime of which he was accused, which involved an axe, a meat grinder and a can of paraffin.

Daniel Hatterson had just raised his fist heavenward and said: "You must see, gentlemen, you must surely *see*, that my client, so pathetically, so tragically, bereft of a sense of right and wrong, a sense most of us God-fearing citizens take for granted, is not capable of comprehending . . ."

It was then that Daniel Hatterson's puzzled face turned a most unpleasant shade of vermilion and he pitched, without further ado, into the jury box. One of the jurors later said he thought Hatterson was throwing himself on the mercy of the court as a last resort.

Marlene went to astronomy club on Thursdays, so she arrived from school late to find the house swarming with various relatives (none of whom she liked), a policeman, the Reverend Collins, and someone with a camera. Her mother greeted her at the door, a box of tissue at the ready, and told her daughter that her father had had an accident at work, that it had been bad, and that Marlene would not be seeing her father again.

"Do you mean he's dead?" asked Marlene, looking past her mother to the house, full of both thick grief and guilty anticipation.

"Yes, darling, he is," said her mother, and she put her hands on Marlene's shoulders in case she wanted to be hugged.

"Did someone kill him?" Marlene was quite accustomed to the occasionally sensational nature of her father's business.

"No. Nothing like that!" Daphne Hatterson's hand went to her swan-like throat, accentuated by a scarf of midnight-black silk with a small pearl brooch pinned to the knot, which softened the unflattering severity of her recently donned mourning dress.

"Well, did he fall or choke or something?" Marlene was not pleased that all these people should know the important facts when she did not. It only served to confirm her feeling of being constantly on the outside of things and set apart.

"No." Daphne glanced over her shoulders at the witnessing friends and relations. Reverend Collins' brow was furrowed. "No, dear. He got sick. A stroke."

"And he's dead." Marlene let the dry, brown leaf of this truth sink to the bottom of her stomach.

"Yes, dear. He died instantly." Daphne watched her daughter, waiting for what she prayed would be tears. She clutched the box of tissues almost hopefully.

"Oh," said Marlene. "Well, that's not exactly an accident, is it? I mean, slipping in a shower is an accident. Getting hit by a bus is an accident. A stroke is more like an act of God." She stared at the reverend, who cleared his throat and slipped away to get more tea.

"Perhaps we'd better get you to your room." As Daphne hustled Marlene up the stairs, she muttered to the friends and relations that it must be shock.

"You should have had word sent to the school," said Marlene, relieved to get away from all those eyes. "It's the least you could have done."

"I just wanted to give you just a few more hours, a few more happy hours, before you had to know . . . Really, darling . . ." Daphne's voice trailed off, unwilling to admit that she hadn't wanted to deal with Marlene until she had support around her, some friends who would ease her through this difficult time.

"Really, indeed," said Marlene.

The funeral was quite the event, a full church and a full house for the buffet afterwards. It was there, as she shadowed behind the potted philodendron, that Marlene heard the specific details of her father's demise whispered among the carrion-crow mourners.

"You know, it was certain he'd lose the case. A man like that – an undeniable monster," said Aunt Lucille, the red of her lipstick bleeding into the deep lines of disapproval around her mouth.

"He couldn't have won it, unless on the grounds of insanity. His only recourse was an emotional plea. Fell in the line of duty, if you ask me," said Aunt Velma.

Marlene promptly decided her father's brain must have exploded from the sheer insanity of it all, and stepping out from her hiding place, promptly said so.

"Well, it was mad, wasn't it?" she said to the astonished faces of her twin paternal aunts. "It was perfectly, utterly crazy to get so worked up about a man who was so bloody minded, so blither-minded himself."

"Marlene, how can you say such a thing?" said Aunt Gloria, who even in mourning wore a proper crinoline and pillbox hat.

Marlene, sturdy and strong even then, never a gazelle of a girl, never coltish as her mother had been, looked her aunt straight in the eye from beneath her blunt brown bangs and said, "I can say it because it's true. Justice was not served. Father should have had more sense than to abandon me in the cause of that *farce*." And she turned heel and ran away, out into the garden where she spent an hour twisting the heads off of the snapdragons and lilies.

Once the funeral was over, the will read, and the clothes packed off to the Salvation Army, they never mentioned Marlene's father again. Daphne thought it was better that way, unaware that the sudden erasure of her father only served to confirm Marlene's suspicions that the things most people took for granted in the world as being solid and trustworthy were not so at all. Daphne mistook the fact that Marlene no longer voiced these opinions as proof she was growing out of them, and saw no reason to stir up the hornet's nest of her daughter's mind. The fact that Marlene had exchanged her fatiguing curiosity for a shell of crusty withdrawal troubled Daphne not at all.

## AN INTERLUDE

Marlene was thirty-nine, and grown into a woman of solitary preferences and social awkwardness. She had tried her hand at study, at academia, but found the curriculum too confining. Recognized by professors and counsellors as having a high level of intelligence (perhaps higher than their own, but they wouldn't admit *that*), her inability to focus or to write an understandable essay, or to follow any sort of direction, saddened them all. They gently suggested she might wish to seek medical assistance, perhaps medication. She declined, with some indignation. She attended college for one year, before dropping out and relinquishing her

dream of a life spent with an eye glued to one the great tel-
escopes of the world. She now supported herself as a typist
in the Department of Geography at the university. The professors gave her things to type – lecture notes, research
papers, and she typed them. Simple and with as little inter-
action as necessary. No one lingered at her desk, which was
in a little back room by itself, to chat, or gossip, or sip coffee.

She still loved the stars, though, and never lost the sense
of awe and peace she found in her days as president of the
school astronomy club. If there was a Plan, a Guiding Hand,
if there was a Presence at Work, then it was not in the con-
fusing daily interactions with other humans, but in the vast,
silent power and majesty of the cosmos. She had a telescope
at the window of her fifth-floor walk-up apartment, which
made the neighbours nervous, but their anxiety was un-
founded. She was interested only in points of light – distant,
cool and still.

Her mother lived across town, but they didn't see each
other any more. Marlene didn't question this. She was only
relieved.

Marlene had no friends, other than Mr. Delillo, who ran
the newsstand on the corner of Walnut and 13th Streets,
and with whom she shared a daily coffee on her way home
from work. She had books. She had movies. She'd had a
boyfriend or two, nothing serious, but she was not a virgin.
There was a brief period when she was in her mid-twenties,
and the world was in the throes of free love and psyche-
delic drugs when her somewhat thick, earthy body and her

strange thoughts were not at odds with fashion and social formula. There was Norman, a skinny digger who lived in a communal squat near the campus, who said her thighs reminded him of the sacred sequoia tree, and he spent nearly two months, high on magic mushrooms and pot, buried between them.

And there was Calvin, an aviation engineer with a middle as loose as a bleached, half-full pillowcase, whom she met at the newsstand. Calvin wooed her by taking her to cheap Italian restaurants full of working men, where Chianti bottles sat on the table with candles stuck in them, and the air was full of smoke.

"I like women who are women, not skinny little girls," he insisted, "and free-thinkers, like you, not mindless unread suburban drones."

He left her, after six months of occasional dinners and three weeks of occasional sex that left her less satisfied than did the *linguini al fredo*, for a woman who formed her political opinions by reading *The Ladies Home Journal* and ate only fish and green vegetables.

The relationships, if they could be called that, had not pleased Marlene, and she was relieved when they ended. In both cases the rituals of reaching out to another's flesh seemed false and contrived. She did not know these men, did not feel connected to them, and did not feel present as they committed the act of love. They were too separate, too Other. Throughout both encounters, she kept most of her thoughts to herself, because she'd learned from her mother this was the best place for her unique perceptions. When they left, it was as though they were not leaving her at all, for she had never been, in her heart, with them.

She had decided she wouldn't try it again, so it was with some surprise that she found herself agreeing to go for coffee with Casper Rachesvsky, who ran the photocopier at the campus print shop. Marlene had liked Casper from the first time they'd met, when she brought a stack of papers to be copied, collated and bound into plastic spines.

She had watched as he used a small machine to punch holes in the paper, his square capable hands tapping the paper this way and that, to make sure all the edges lined up properly. The punched-out confetti spilled off to the floor.

"You'd think someone would find a way to save all those bits and squoosh 'em up into new paper. Lost confetti is like a wedding that never happened," she said, mostly to herself, not expecting an answer.

Casper replied, "I used to have a cocker spaniel named Poirot. When I brushed her I thought there should be a way to save the fur and make yarn out of it. Knit myself a sweater. Softest thing I ever felt." What might be a *non sequitur* to others made perfect sense to Marlene.

"People don't see the obvious," she tried, just to see if he'd answer.

"Obviously," he said, and that was all. He looked at her, his face serious and direct, as though he understood her distress with both conversation and silence. Marlene felt a faint stir of something like recognition under the flat shield of her breastbone.

Casper and Marlene began to have a friendly, bantering sort of talk whenever she came by the photocopy centre, which she found herself doing more often. They were exactly the same height, with the same barrel chests, square faces and straight brown hair. Someone once asked if they were brother and sister. They said no, but later shared the possibility that it might, through some bizarre adoption conspiracy, be so.

Casper had neither more friends, nor experience in matters of love, than Marlene did, which she also found reassuring. Being with Casper was as relaxing as being with herself.

## SOMETIME IN THE MIDDLE OF THINGS

Marlene was forty-three and married to the man of, if not her dreams, at least her heart's kindling, when her world took an irrevocable plunge into bleak solitude.

Marlene and Casper lay in bed in the early morning hours, awake, but not talking. Casper seemed vague and preoccupied, as he had done for some months now. Distant. He withheld himself and she didn't know why. This was new. They had been married only two years. The first eighteen months had been the best of Marlene's life. She felt she had at last found a person with whom she could share herself. They were so similar there had been no great chasm to be crossed.

Marlene tried to rouse him from his fugue by running her fingers along the inside of his thigh, as she knew he liked, but he pushed her hand away.

He inhaled once. And then again. The sort of inhalations which signal a sentence is trying to make its way to the surface of the lips, but is fighting headwinds. Marlene waited. Finally he spoke. But what he said made very little sense. The words were related to nothing, were connected to nothing in the life Marlene and Casper shared, the only life she believed either of them was living.

He said these words: "I love Brian."

This small sentence confused Marlene. For one thing, she didn't know any Brian and for another, what Casper could possibly intend by saying this was a mystery.

"What does that mean?" she asked.

Casper turned his back, swinging his large legs from the side of the bed, planting his big feet on the wooden floor. He put his hands to his head, his thumbs alongside his cheekbones, his fingers over his eyebrows, as though he was trying to see something a long way away.

"It means . . . it means I love him. I've tried to stop . . . seeing him, but I can't. I'm very sorry. You don't know how sorry."

"What does *that* mean?" She wanted to keep him talking until she understood how this information, dropped into their bed without warning, like a spider from the ceiling, would alter them.

"I was wrong to try and live this way. A lie. I should have told you. This is tearing me apart." He pounded the bones above his eyes with the heels of his hands, hard enough to jar, but not, Marlene noticed, to hurt too much. "I've tried so hard, Marlene." He turned and the look on his face was frightening, because it transformed Casper's face into a face Marlene didn't recognize. "I wanted a life with you. I care about you. But this isn't fair to either of us."

*Isn't fair?* No. This wasn't fair, to say these things, to begin a day this way.

Marlene's mind tried to examine the thin cobweb of information, but it kept breaking apart. She held her breath. She felt her heart in its cage of bones begin to flail about. She looked down at her body, lying still as a corpse under the lightweight summer blanket. Her body was thick and sturdy and compact, and for a moment she could not attach her interior self to it. Knowledge and understanding, twins twisted as serpents, slithered to her throat. They opened their mouths, unhinged their jaws to take her in. Her mind scattered for protection, clung tightly to nothing. She would not breathe.

Even as she clutched this still space, she knew the stillness would not last. She knew she would have to breathe eventually, and that with breath would come the beginning of the knowing time, the understanding, and the agony.

She held her lungs still as long as possible, shutting off her throat, until the beating of her floundering heart pushed open her lips and dragged the air down. Knife air, lava air, blood-thick air in her throat, filling up every pocket of her being. Her body swelled with incoming air until there was no place left for it to go but out again. Out it went, in a long keening, a banshee of breath, the sound of her world rending, ripping.

"You're leaving me! Leaving me! You don't want me!"

Marlene looked at Casper, crying now and a stranger to her. Apparently, he had always been a stranger to her. In this, the most fundamental of judgments, she had been wrong. If she was wrong about this, she was wrong about everything. She was not to be trusted. He was not to be trusted. No one. Nothing could be trusted.

Casper reached for her hand. She raised her own and slapped him. Not an open-handed slap, the slap of a woman scorned, but a raised-up, half-closed, back-handed fist-slug that began when she crossed her right hand towards her left shoulder, near her heart, and with all the force in her bovine limbs, she clocked him. Casper huffed, that was what the sound was, not a cry or a yell or a mousy little OW, but a passive huff, one might almost interpret as indignation. Casper huffed as Marlene hit him, and fell from the bed to the floor.

Marlene realized she was standing, must have stood as the air filled her, as it lifted her above the marriage bed. Casper stayed on the floor, which was both cowardly and wise. Marlene wanted only to be gone.

She pushed her legs into pants and socks and shoes, her breasts into a sturdy white cotton brassiere and her arms, shoulders, chest into a sweatshirt. She plunged down the steps, flung open the door to the apartment that was no longer her home. She took her brittle heart in her hands, carried it out of the building, down the steps onto the street, and set out. She didn't know where. She didn't care. She would not be back.

Disoriented and highly charged, Marlene was struck by the acute clarity of her vision. She wondered if her mind was searching for tiny details to hold onto in an effort to survive. Or perhaps her mind, having been freed of all distracting illusions, was at last coming into its own power. It didn't matter. Without her heart, she would not last. A heart so crushed would be unable to survive in the long run, that much was clear. But in the horrible sucking breath of the aftershock, she was filled with a sense of the piercing purity of all things. The colour of the cement in the sidewalk was the colour of the sea on a stormy day. The green of the grass was the colour of emeralds. Each leaf on the oak tree was outlined precisely, the work of a fine lace maker. The vapour of the clouds was both transparent and luminous. A child sat on the sidewalk and played with a thin-waisted, long-legged, headless doll. Each detail of the child's overalls, the silver buttons, the stitching on the seams, the dusty knees, the peach-juice stain, everything the eye normally skimmed over was now clearly visible. The child itself was a source of so many nuances of colour and texture and shape that Marlene had to look away, or be consumed with studying her. The houses on the street were painted not orange, but nectarine, not green, but sea foam. The world was outlined in a draftsman's pen line. It was numinous, each infinitesimal blade of grass and insect wing a testament to some Divine Plan of which she was not a part.

Marlene felt the load, and shift, and correction of her entire body on each foot with every stop she took. She felt over-weighted, like a thing usually water-buoyed, now suffocated under the load of heavy, grief-sodden air. She moved her hands slowly back and forth in front of her, as though warding something off, or pushing something back.

A man and woman, elderly, lumpy, and bland as mashed potatoes, walked towards her. The woman's vein-traced hand lay on her husband's arm, his burled fingers held an aluminium cane. They gave her a wide berth, averted their eyes, and instinctively drew closer to one another. Marlene took this as right and fair. She assumed a posture of dignity in the hurricane's eye surrounding the wild abandon of mourning.

She was aware of a sensation in her chest not unlike she imagined it would feel to be clawed by a bear. A small part of her, a fragment cast off by the power of her thrashing emotions, stood to the side and calmly noted, with only the faintest twinge of anxiety, that whatever she had been before, she was becoming something different now. She was bear-found. Bear bait.

Marlene walked through morning. Marlene walked through afternoon.

Marlene with a great white bear stalking her bleeding self, sniffing at the air for her scent of separation and following the trail of isolation across the ice forming around her.

The clawing of a bear. That was what it felt like. The bear was both her breaking heart and the breaker *of* her heart. Both herself and her destroyer. With every heartbeat the bear swatted his stone-heavy claws deeper. She was ice-trapped. The bear was her only witness, her only executioner.

*Savsaat.* The Inuit called it *savsaat.* The entrapment. Beluga whale in ice. When the weather betrays the whale, and tricks her with mild temperatures into thinking she's safe to approach land. Then the heartless freeze. Freak freeze. Friendless freeze. The whale is imprisoned far from free flowing water. She must huddle by any hole in the ice she can find, hoping to survive until a thaw. Knowing it is lost, all lost, forever lost, but what choice does she have, forced by a wicked creator to breathe for life?

A polar bear can smell a trapped whale ten miles away. The bear comes, lethal and inevitable. The bear sits smug and warm in its deceptive fur, not white, but transparent, a greenhouse of fur, and waits for the smooth, pale skin of the whale to rise. The bear pounds a razor-embedded sledge-hammer, just there on the blowhole. Tender, as openings to the interior of a creature always are. The whale is out of choices. Soon she will suffocate, her airway shredded. She will suffocate at the surface; she will drown if she dives to the cool depths, pink as rose petals now.

Think of the hideous strength of the bear, to drag a whale from water. Think of the terror of the whale's choices: death by suffocation, drowning or being eaten alive.

*We are what we eat*, thought Marlene. *But if we are the eaten then, don't we also become the eater?* Marlene knew she had been the whale, swimming in the illusion of a boundless, benevolent sea. But everything, she now understood, was mere glamour. All her life she had felt that the under-pinning, the girders in the foundation of the world, were uncertain. But Casper, whom she'd taken as kin, had made sense of her world. His sturdy compact body was her twin, male-born. Touching him had been like touching herself so she had no shyness with him. They had agreed on their direction, neither too fast nor too slow, neither too high nor too low, neither too near nor too far. They would take a middling path, but take it together. They had, she thought, both been relieved to fall towards the other.

It had been the one incontrovertible thing.

If this were not true, then nothing was true. She could believe nothing. Trust nothing. Be joined with nothing. She would be safe only apart. Away from. By full nightfall, it was decided. It would be her life's work, to have as little connection as possible, for her judgment could not be trusted. She would forever be wrong. She would stay alone, neither in spite, nor in a cry for pity, but because it was her nature. Bears are like that.

## ALTERNATE PERSPECTIVE, IN A DIFFERENT VOICE

A woman holds out her hand to Sylvia.

"Spare change." Not a question.

The woman is maybe in her late fifties and hard packed as thirsty earth. Sylvia squints into a glare of yellow T-shirt, taut across an imposing chest. A black baseball cap sits firmly on straight brown hair, threaded with grey. Pressed khaki shorts. A black and purple gym bag slung over one shoulder. The waistband, with loops but no belt, is at the level of Sylvia's nose.

Again. "Spare change," in a voice free of entreaty, full of entitlement.

"Ignore her," says Harry. Harry wears a blue shirt and exact-match tie. He has picked this terrace restaurant, deemed it chic enough to celebrate the done-deal.

The hand is in the air above Sylvia's salad. Cleaner than you would expect such a hand to be, and firm, fixed in the air without a quiver. There are bruises along the outside of the arms, bruises of various size and colour, some new and some old. Sylvia feels frightened, looking at those bruises and imagining all sorts of things, all kinds of vulnerabilities that women share.

"Gimme a dollar," says the woman, who does not look vulnerable, never mind the bruises. She looks at Sylvia placidly, taking her in (blond hair, blouse the colour of a robin's egg, skirt the colour of rain) as though she was no more real than a billboard advertisement. If there is judgment in the woman's gaze, it does not alter the tone of her voice, which remains vaguely fatigued and detached, as if she has been having the same conversation all day. It reminds Sylvia of the tone her mother used to take when, as a child, she was caught chewing gum. "Give me the gum," her mother would say, hand extended for Sylvia to spit into, her mother weary of having to say it *again.*

"Go. Away," says Harry, with space between the words, as if speaking to a simpleton or a person unaccustomed to English.

"Harry, give her something."

"Where the hell is the waiter?" says Harry.

The woman stands too close to Sylvia, so close she can feel the heat from her square body and smell her scent. She smells of something a little musty, not unclean exactly, but like something that has been hidden in an attic and absorbed dust and distance and memory. It is a smell at odds with the bright sunny horizon of her T-shirted chest. The woman heaves the gym bag to the ground. It lands next to her sneakered foot with a heavy thud.

"Gimme *two* dollars," says the woman.

"Now, look here . . ." Harry's blue tie now looks rather tight around his reddening neck and draws attention to the dark nick where he cut himself shaving this morning.

"Pass me my purse," says Sylvia, reaching to the window ledge behind Harry where she put her bag for safekeeping.

"Don't be ridiculous. This is blackmail." Harry, his face hard, looks for the waiter, who stands next to a table twenty feet away. He glances in their direction, but quickly drops his eyes. Sylvia reaches for her purse, but Harry takes her wrist.

"Sylvia, no."

"Give the woman a dollar and let's get on with our meal."

"*Two* dollars," the woman corrects them.

"Bloody beggars are everywhere. Get the hell away from this table!" Harry does not relinquish his grasp on Sylvia's arm.

The hand moves closer to Sylvia's face. She can see the pulse in the woman's sunburned wrist.

Sylvia wrenches from Harry's grip and grabs for her purse. Under the scorch of his glare, she finds two dollars.

"There you go." She puts the money in the woman's hand. The skin feels rough and cool, like soft wood pulp.

The woman picks up her bag and moves a few tables over. She stares at two men, who do their best not to meet her eyes.

"Gimme a dollar," she says.

"You see, not even a thank you," says Harry.

As the woman walks away, Sylvia sees shadows that may be bruises along the backs of her legs, and a large purple varicose vein. She looks down at her plate of seafood risotto, full of plump, rosy little shrimps and perfect rings of squid. She starts to pick up her fork, but then puts it down.

"Drink your champagne," she says to Harry.

### AN AFTERWORD

Marlene closes the door behind her, her pockets clinking and weighted with change. She puts her gym bag by the entrance, turns and locks the door with both chain and deadbolt. There is a hot plate on the counter with a hardened crust of food fried. On a shelf: cans of corn, beans, tinned meat, and condensed milk. A small table and a chair, covered with yellow T-shirts, all yellow, stand under the single window. Three *National Geographic* magazines lie on the floor, tattered and water-swollen. A piled nest of blankets, but no sheets, adorns a double bed, sagging in the centre. An outdated calendar is tacked on the wall, sporting a picture of earth taken from space. Around the window, red and green Christmas lights hang. There is a small blue bureau, with a drawer missing. Marlene goes to the sink and finds her glass, foggy with fingerprints, runs water from the tap and drinks.

She turns back to her gym bag, and pulls out something wrapped in a towel. She sits on the bed – the springs complain – and she unwraps a stone statue, the size of a loaf of bread. It is her treasure. She carries it with her everywhere. Marlene found the statue in Our Lady of the Consolation Church, into which she'd ducked to avoid a rainstorm two years ago. The treasure stood on the floor by the rectory door. The head was broken off, leaving only a body with a rod of metal sticking up from the neck. Marlene was sure it was a saint, and, because of the lamb by one leg and the wolf by the other, she decided it was St. Francis. Both animals gaze in adoration at the place where once the face had been. No bear, but she was sure St. Francis would bless the bears too.

Marlene had pitied the decapitated, abandoned saint. She also considered it was a sign, her finding it that way, although she wasn't sure of what. She had picked it up, felt the heft in her hand, the cool of the stone, the smoothness of its surface. She liked the feel of it. Liked the look of the small animals, cunningly carved. Without another thought, she put it in her gym bag, and left the church.

That night when she got home, she took the statue in her hands, and fancied it warmed to her touch. It was such a solid thing. She stared and stared at it, especially at the small hands, held out in benediction and compassion to the heads of the lamb and the wolf. Did the fingers move? Marlene lifted the statue to her cheek, ran the statue against her skin. Did it tingle? She ran the statue over her neck, her chest, her right arm, her left. Marlene smiled, felt a laugh bubble up to her lips.

It became her ritual, this application of stone. In this way, she communed with the saint. To what end she performed this ritual was unclear. Perhaps for healing, but she didn't feel sick, perhaps for salvation, although she didn't feel damned. She only knew that it became necessary, that she had to do it, in the same way she had to lock the doors, keep the Christmas lights in the window, eat off only green plates, and never let the blankets on the bed *ever* touch the floor.

It took some time to realize that the more relish with which she applied the stone to her skin, the more benefits it bestowed.

Now, Marlene pats the stone against her arms, her neck, her head, her cheek, her back, her feet, her right leg, her left. As she taps the stone against her skin, her flesh becomes warm and pink and glowing. She increases the force of each blow, feels the energy from the headless saint go deeper into her. The sensations begin. She feels the heat. Hits herself harder.

Marlene bends back her head, exposes her throat to the stone. The boundaries between where she ends and where the world begins soften, shift, and for a sweet, timeless moment, dissolve.

# IN THE MEMORY HOUSE

Becky's mother played solitaire on the coffee table. A Matinee cigarette dangled delicately from her lower lip. Now and then, she sipped from her glass of scotch and ginger ale. She wore black Mary Tyler Moore Capri pants and the pale yellow sweater with the buttons made out of red plastic cherries, which was a favourite of Becky's father. Becky, who was six years and five months old, watched *Chez Helene* on the TV and tried to learn French.

Becky listened very carefully, and repeated *"bonjour"* and *"crayon."* She knew she could remember that meant pencil. She wanted to be able to speak French by the time her father came home, because her mother had told her he was in Paris on business and that Paris was in another country called France and that was where they spoke French all the time. She wondered how she would put the word pencil into a sentence for her father.

She heard his key in the door and jumped up.

"Hey! Bon-jer! Where are my girls?" he called out as he threw open the front door. A blast of wet and icy Canadian wind picked up the solitaire cards and scattered them.

"Daddy! Daddy! Not Bon-jer! Bon*jour*! You said it wrong. Say Bon*jour*!" Becky said, as he dropped his bags and scooped her up into his arms, up so high she could touch the light fixture on the ceiling if she wanted to. But she didn't want to. She just wanted to put her hands on his face, on either side of his big face, and feel the bristly roughness of his skin.

"Hi, there, Miss Smartie Pants, you been a good girl?"

"Yes, I have, I have. You can ask Mommy."

He put her down and she hugged his leg while he greeted his wife.

"I missed you," he said and hugged Becky's mother.

"Good trip?" She offered only her cheek for kissing.

"Busy. Very busy."

"Must have been."

"I tried to get a minute to call, but you wouldn't believe the way these Frenchies go on. Yack, yack, yack. Meetings all day, all night. Barely had a minute to grab a shower and a couple of hours' sleep. Damn near killed me! But it paid off. We got the deal, even if I didn't have a minute to myself. Besides, I didn't want to spend all the money on long distance."

"I know." Becky's mother took his coat as he shrugged it off and went to the closet to hang it up. "But I worry, you know, when I don't hear from you at all. I even thought of calling the hotel one night."

"Really? Well, you probably wouldn't have found me there. We were in meetings 'til all hours, one night 'til nearly four a.m., would you believe it?"

"Daddy, what did you bring us? Were you too busy for presents?"

"I was awfully busy . . ."

"But not too busy?"

"Well . . ."

"Oh, Daddy!"

"I might just have a thing or two."

Becky clapped her hands and ran to the bags he had dropped by the door.

"Where is it?"

"Hold on just a minute, Becky, for heaven's sake," her mother said. "Go sit on the couch and give your father a minute to catch his breath before you start grabbing for things."

Becky ran to the couch and flopped on it, bouncing. She knew her mother was excited too. Her father always came back from trips with presents – chocolate and stuffed animals and once a bathing cap with a big flower on the top. She loved that bathing cap so much that even though it was mid-winter when she received it, Becky wore it the next day right along with her snowsuit and mittens.

Her father started pulling stuff out of his suitcase, rumpled shirts and socks and underwear.

"Now, I know it's in here somewhere."

"You're just like Marco Polo," her mother said.

"Who's that?" Becky asked.

"A great explorer who spent far too much time away from home, who tried to make everything better when he returned by bribing his family with presents."

"Phyllis!" her father said, clutching his cheeks in mock horror. "Could it be you don't want any presents?"

"I didn't say that."

"That's good, because none of my other girlfriends suit this colour." He winked at Becky and passed a package wrapped in pale blue tissue paper to Becky's mother.

"Oh, Frank, it's absolutely beautiful." She wrapped the silk scarf around her shoulders and ran her fingers over the material. It was white with little blue Eiffel towers scattered all over it and the word "Paris" written in what looked like gold braid around the outside to form a border.

"That's real silk, you know, all the way from gay Paree!"

"It's just lovely!" She leaned over the table and gave Frank, who sat on the floor, a big kiss.

"But Madame, there's more!" he cried and produced another package from the magic bag. "Perfume for my lady."

"This is really too much," said her mother, although she plucked it from his hand in a flash. Inside was a small bottle of the most mystical deep blue colour with a silver stopper. "Evening in Paris! Oh, I've always wanted Evening in Paris! I love it. I love *you!*"

"Enough to get us a drink?"

"Oh, I suppose so. But just one, I've got to finish dinner."

As she walked past him he reached out and slapped her behind, causing her to squeal and laugh as she hopped off into the kitchen, one hand rubbing the sore spot.

"What about me?" Becky pleaded, hands clasped under her chin, and shoulders hunched with anticipation.

"Let's wait 'til your mother comes back in."

"Mom! Hurry up! Hurry!"

"Oh, good grief, Becky!" Phyllis came back into the room, holding two full glasses. "Okay, okay, I'm here. Here, baby." She handed one to Frank, who took three big gulps and nearly emptied it.

"Ah!" He smacked his lips and put the glass down. "Now, what could there be in here for Becky? Did I forget it? Gee whiz, maybe I forgot it on the plane." He reached deep into his bag, almost up to his shoulder.

"Oh no. Oh, Daddy!" Becky's heart fell to her knees and her stomach flipped.

"No, it's all right, here it is!" Her father held out an oblong package. She reached for it. "Careful, now, careful. That's very delicate. And it's heavy."

"Put it down on the table, Sweetie," said her mother.

Becky's pudgy little fingers went to work ripping away the pink paper. It was heavy. She peeled back the final layer and then opened the lid of the box underneath. "Ooooohhhhh . . ." she breathed. It was too lovely. Too wonderful.

"Let me help you." Her mother pulled the heavy object up out of the box and placed it on the table. "Oh, Frank, where did you find this?"

It was a champagne bottle, and in the bottle was champagne, of course, and Becky knew what that was because she'd seen her parents drink it on their wedding anniversary. But floating in the champagne were flecks of gold, tumbling and swirling just like the snow in the little water-filled dome with the snowman inside her grandmother gave her last year. But this was so much better! Because in the bottom was a tiny porcelain dancing girl, wearing a white foamy tutu and standing on tiny gold ballet slippers, way up on her toes. It was a thing more precious, more magical, more perfect than anything Becky had ever seen.

"Here, give it to me, let me show you," said her father. He picked it up and turned it over. Her father fiddled with a small knob on the bottom. Then he set it down on the coffee table and as he did, strains of the most beautiful music ever heard by anyone began to play. At the same time, the little woman in the golden rain began to turn round and round and round, dancing in the fairy kingdom inside the bottle. Becky was afraid she might cry it was so pretty.

"What do you say, Becky?" prodded her mother.

"Oh, Daddy, thank you, thank you, thank you! It's the best thing I've ever had. The best thing I've ever seen. It's my favourite thing forever, I promise." Becky jumped up and ran around the table, careful not to knock it and jar the music box, and threw her arms around her father's neck, smothering him with kisses, all over his eyes and nose and cheeks and chin and not even minding the smell of the whiskey.

He hugged her back, and grinned and laughed, and her mother laughed and they were all very happy.

"More drinks, I say! More drinks! I think this calls for a celebration!" Frank said, and Phyllis smiled and went to get the whiskey bottle.

All through dinner, Becky kept running back to peek at the dancer in the bottle. She discovered a little switch on the side that turned the music on and off, once it was wound up, which was good, because it meant she didn't have to keep turning the bottle over. It was very heavy and she was afraid she'd drop it. She could have spent the rest of her life gazing at that bottle.

When she went to bed, her mother made her leave the music box in the living room because she said she didn't want Becky staying up all night playing with it. After all, she had school the next day. She fell asleep with her stuffed bunny under one arm and dreamed dreams of gold-starred skies and toe shoes.

In the morning, first thing, before her mother had even come in to wake her, Becky, wearing her footed, flap-door jammies, rushed into the living room. Bunny trailed ear-held along the floor. She couldn't wait to introduce Bunny to the dancing lady.

The coffee table was music box bare. Her mother must have put it away somewhere. Becky went into the kitchen and found her mother sitting at the chrome table in her old stained housecoat, drinking coffee and smoking a cigarette.

"Where's my dancer?" she said.

"Don't you even say good morning?"

"Good morning," she was impatient. "Mummy, where'd you put it?"

"Put what?"

"Mummy, don't tease." Teasing wasn't fair. Not about something this important. "Where's Daddy's present?"

"You broke it," she said.

"Broke it?" She pulled Bunny up to her stomach and hugged him.

"Yes."

"No, I didn't. I didn't." Becky's heart pounded. "Where is it?!"

"Don't you remember? You knocked it off the coffee table last night."

Her mother flicked the ash off the end of her cigarette and looked into her coffee cup for a moment. Then she looked up, directly at Becky and said it again.

"You broke it."

She looked at her mother. Becky's eyebrows pulled down over her nose. What was happening? Her chin began to tremble. Something burned in her chest, under the blue kitty appliqué on her jammies. Her hands formed very small fists. She opened her mouth. Then she closed it. A huge lump moved in her throat. She opened her mouth again.

"That's a lie, that's a lie, a lie!" she screamed over and over.

Her mother said nothing.

Becky fell into a great rushing cyclone of sound, wailing tears, and a terrible deep tearing. Her head shook and her arms and legs and hands and feet; all of her flew off in all directions, as though she was being blown up, blown apart. She couldn't stop shrieking at her dry-eyed, coffee-sipping mother.

Later, when she was allowed to come out of her room, where she had had to stay if she was going to act that way, if she was going to work herself up into such a state she couldn't even go to school, she found the thing. Trash can buried. Even the dancer smashed. Next to the empty whiskey bottles. The muscles in her neck tightened, and her eyes began to sting again. She found it very hard to breathe.

She ran a finger along the delicate porcelain leg and the teeny foot in the gold shoe, still attached to the base. The broken edge was sharp and a drop of blood appeared on the tip of her finger. She put her finger in her mouth. Then, she put the garbage can lid back down. She left the shattered dancer in there.

That was a long time ago, when they lived in the house with the blue roof. They referred to it like that, as though the roof being blue conferred some sort of spiritual sky-kissed status to the shabby little bungalow. *The Blue Roof,* they'd say, *that happened when we lived in The Blue Roof.* There were lots of stories to tell, about how extremely happy they'd been then. And there were certain stories they did not tell, like this one.

# RAT MEDICINE

I saw the first rat next to where we stored the chicken feed. It was a week before John used his fists on me. I was out by the sacks and felt like somebody was watching me. The hair stood up on places of my body where I didn't know I had hair. I put down the tin pail I used to scatter the feed and picked up a shovel leaning against the shed. We'd never had no trouble. Living so far out of town like we did, criminal types didn't seem to have the gumption to haul ass all the way out to our place, but there was always a first time. I turned around and there he was, sitting back on his hindquarters like a little rat dog begging for a tidbit, up on the shed roof. Bold as brass, he didn't flick a whisker. He just kept looking at me, his little front paws tucked up in front of his belly, his eyes bright as black glass.

"What do you think you're doing up there?" But, of course, the rat didn't say nothing back. "Don't think you can get in and eat up all this good feed." The rat kept looking at me, straight and firm like. "We got a big old tomcat round here. He's going to be picking his teeth with your bones, my friend." If rats could be said to smirk, that's what he was doing.

Now, most people, they really hate rats. Not me. I don't hate anything about the animal kingdom. Not snakes, not spiders, not coyote, not buzzard. That's the Ojibway blood, from my mother's people. My granny used to tell me, you dream about a rat, you dreaming about some sickness, maybe a bad one, soon to come on. Granny was usually right about these things. I set store in omens, in symbols and signs. It's all there if you know what to look for. So I looked at the rat, recognized it for a fellow who'd come to tell me something.

"You got news for me, rat man? If you do, you better tell me. I ain't got all day."

The rat cleaned behind his ears. Then he turned and stuck his bald tail straight in the air and disappeared toward the other side of the shed roof. I tried to get around to see where he was going, fast as my size would allow, but when I looked there weren't no sign of him.

I didn't tell John about the rat because I knew he'd just blame it on me. Tell me I didn't keep the place clean enough. Which was a lie, but true facts never matter much to John when he got a good rage going. I got a couple of old oil drums John kept about the place and put the sacks of feed in there, put old boards on the top and weighted them down with rocks.

When John came back that night, he was in a mood even fouler than the night before. His moods had been getting worse for some time. He slammed the screen door so hard I thought the wood frame'd splinter.

"Nell!" he yelled. "This place looks like a goddamn pigsty! What the hell do you do all day?"

There wasn't no point in answering. "C'mon in here and get your dinner, John."

He sat down at the kitchen table. His filthy work boots left muddy prints on my clean floor. He stank of sweat from working at the mill in this heat. 'Course he wouldn't have thought to wash up before dinner. I didn't dare say nothing. I served us both up our food and set the plates down on the table.

"Fat as you are," John said, "don't think you're going to be eating all that. Take half off, Nell. You need to lose some goddamn weight."

I just looked at him.

"I mean it. You are getting to be a big fat squaw. I can't hardly bear to look at you."

I am a big woman, I don't deny it. I wasn't always this size, though I never have been small. It was after John Jr. died that I really started packing it on. Seemed like I didn't want to do much more than try and fill up the hole his dying left. Slipped away in his sleep, silent as a leaf falling in the dark, and him not a year old. But I found a way to keep going without turning mean, turning against the force of life. Which is more than I can say for his father. We'd lost the baby more'n three years then and John never did get over it.

That and the farm failing.

John said the reason the farm failed, why the crops all withered up and got ate by every sort of crawling creature, was the land was poison. Said the poison came from up the mine when the company started digging great wounds in the side of South Mountain. Well, I don't know. Maybe yes, and maybe no. It wasn't that John didn't work hard, it's just he never had his father's touch. Everything just turned to rot as soon as he came near it. It made him bitter.

The worst was last month, when we couldn't make the mortgage. It hurt his pride, faced with the choice to go down to Rickett's Mill and beg for work, or hand over the land that'd been in his family for generations to the bank. It was hard on a man, sure hard. Years of too little money and too much whiskey and a small town where a man could never get ahead of his reputation. John liked his whiskey more and more. Me, I never touched the stuff. My mother and grandmother both impressed on me that you didn't get to be no spirit walker with a bottle in your hand. That might be okay for whites, but it wasn't for Indians. They don't call it "spirits" for nothing, and these weren't the good kind.

So I tried to be understanding with John. That's the way women are, I think, that's the medicine we carry. To try to understand a man and stay soft about it. Water medicine, going around the rock, slowly smoothing out the rough spots. But that don't mean the hurts aren't there, deep in the marrow.

I looked across the table and saw the contempt in his face. I scraped half my food off my plate, but it didn't matter. I'd lost my appetite anyway.

That night I dreamed about a rat. It was sitting on the roof, like some sort of weather vane. It faced east and its nose scented every little breeze that came along.

Three days later, I was washing dishes, up to my arms in warm, soap-creamy water. I like washing dishes; it's like meditation, just looking out the window at the back garden. That year I'd put in nasturtiums, because I like their peppery taste and they look so pretty. I got a crop of the three sisters: corn, beans and squash, plus tomatoes, zucchini, carrots and such, set about with a border of marigolds to keep down the bugs. I have a good hand at gardens, although I don't brag about it, because it sets John off to distraction the way things just seem to jump to life under my fingers.

So anyway, there I am, looking out the window and day-dreaming about the sorts of things a woman daydreams about when her man don't want to touch her anymore, and I realize there's a face in the window looking back at me. A rat face. There's the bugger, just sitting on the windowsill, staring me down. His fur's all clean and glossy brown and he's got a white stomach and little pink ears. He reaches out and puts one little paw up against the glass. I put my finger up against the glass on my side. He doesn't budge and the two of us stay like that for a minute or so, like some-body visiting a prisoner in a jail, although it was hard to figure out who was who. I had half a mind to open the window up and let him in; I was almost getting fond of the little guy.

Oscar, our tomcat and mouser supreme, lay out on the warm stones. He stretched himself into one of those con-tortions only cats can do, all sinew and pretzel.

"You better get gone, little buddy," I said to the rat. The rat just looked at me and put both paws up on the window.

I tapped on the glass, trying to scare him off. Oscar often jumped up on the sill so I could open the window and let him in, and I didn't want to see the little guy get eaten up. "Go on! Go on!" I flicked my fingers, trying not to draw Oscar's attention. Too late. Oscar hightailed it over, ready to pounce on the rat. I closed my eyes.

Next thing, I heard Oscar's whining meow, demanding I let him in. I opened my eyes, figuring the rat had taken a quick dive out of there. On one end of the ledge was Oscar, as expected, but on the other end, not a foot away, was the rat. Calm as a cream-fed cat himself, eyes directly on me. Oscar didn't even notice. I opened the window to let Oscar in, wondering if the rat planned on jumping in as well, but he stayed put. Oscar scattered in, upsetting a glass left to dry on the drain board. I dove to grab it before it fell to the floor. When I turned back, the rat was gone. I shook my head and looked at Oscar.

"Well, some fine hunter you are, you big hairball." Oscar looked at me with the same complete lack of interest he always does, unless there's fish guts involved.

That night, John threw his plate of food over my head where it shattered into a hundred pieces. Said I'd burned the chops, which was nonsense. He shoved me up against the counter and smeared a dishrag in my face. Told me to clean it up and fix him something decent to eat. By the time I cleaned it up and cooked him some new chops, crying all the while, he'd passed out in the La-Z-Boy in front of the TV with a bottle of Jack Daniels in his fist. I put a blanket over him and left him there.

That night I dreamed a swarm of rats churned under our bed, their tails all tied together in knots.

In the morning, I had a big purple bruise on my hip from where I connected with the counter. I had five small, separate storm-cloud coloured bruises on my upper arm. As I fixed John coffee and eggs and didn't talk to him at all, he came up behind me and, seeing the marks, kissed every one of them and said he was sorry. His damp lips felt so good on my parched skin.

"I'm sorry, baby, I'm sorry," he kept muttering. I could have sworn he shed a tear.

John is a good-looking man. The first time I saw him, coming to buy smoked fish off my Uncle Joe, and me only eighteen at the time, I was a goner. This big old cowboy in the skin-tight jeans was the one for me. Looked just like Clint Eastwood. Auntie Betty said I was crazy to go off and marry some white man. We didn't know his family stories, didn't know what kind of past he was hauling around with him. But I didn't care. My eyes were focused firmly on his round little white man's butt in those Levi's.

"I don't know why you put up with me sometimes," he said, and cradled my face in his big callused hands. He said he was sorry again and took me in his arms right there in the kitchen. I forgave him. You bet I did.

Two days later I was sitting in the kitchen having coffee with my friend Joelle when I look up over her shoulder to the top of the refrigerator, and what do I see but my rat pal looking out at me from in between the fat chef cookie jar and the empty plastic ice cube trays.

"I'll be damned. Joelle, turn around slow and look up on the top of the fridge."

"What?" she said.

"Up there, look! Look at that damn rat!"

"Rat!" she shrieked. "What rat?"

"There, right there – look at it!"

"What are you talking about? I don't see no rat."

"You don't see him. Right there. That rat?" The rat sat up on his haunches, spit into his paws and gave himself a good old cleaning.

"Where are you looking?"

"There, goddamnit! Washing his ears!"

"I don't know what you're smoking, but there is no rat on the refrigerator. You're giving me the creeps."

Now there were two of them. Something caught my eye. I looked over by the sink and there was another one.

"You don't see anything at all strange in this kitchen?" I asked.

"The only strange thing in this kitchen is *you*."

When Joelle left, I called over to the rez. I called my Auntie Betty.

"I got rat problems." I said.

"You got rats," Auntie Betty said, practical as always, "you got to go out to the field they live in and explain to them you ain't got no extras to go round but you'll try and leave them out some of what you can spare if they agree to respect your stores."

"Ain't that kind of rat," I said.

"Well, what kind are they?"

"The kind only I can see. And I been dreaming about them, too."

"Oh. That kind of rat." She paused. "I'll call you back."

I knew she was going to go pray some and ask her spirits what was going on over at my place. I'm not as good at this direct stuff as she is. I drank two more cups of tea waiting for the phone to ring.

"You got problems in your house, eh?" she said. "You got marriage problems."

"Yeah, I know."

"He's got some bad stuff around him. Very dark stuff."

I didn't say anything. I remembered the look on his face when he threw the plate.

"He's got anger twisted up in him, that one. You got to be careful. You know what I mean?"

"What should I do?"

"What you asking me that for? You gonna listen to me? You gonna come back home? You gonna leave that white man?"

I didn't answer.

"Uh-huh," Auntie Betty said. "I thought so. Okay, now you listen to me. Animals don't take the time out of their busy day unless they got serious business. You hear me?"

"I hear."

"You got to listen to them. You got a bad sickness coming into your house. You need to clear things out. I don't know if it's too far-gone, but you got to smudge out your house good. You got sweetgrass? You got sage?"

"Yeah."

"Well, use 'em. Smoke that house up good, smoke your bed up good. Put a red blanket on the bed."

"Okay."

"Then you go get these plants and boil 'em up. Drink the tea." She named some herbs and plants.

"One thing, Nell, one thing I got to ask. Is he hitting you?"

"Naw. Not really."

"What the hell is 'not really!' Either he is, or he ain't! You better get ready. His anger's gonna bust out all over you. I'll do what I can, but I don't know. You should come home for a while."

"I can't. I love him, Auntie."

"Love! Phooey! Should go back to the old ways! Let your aunties pick you out a good red man. Stay where we can keep an eye on you! You young people! All the same!" She went on for a while, but I didn't listen much. I knew this part by heart. Besides, I was too busy watching the rats run back and forth from the bedroom to the bathroom.

"Nell? You listening?"

"Yes, Auntie."

"Okay, one last thing. Fat as you are these days, you ain't gonna be able to dodge him if he comes at you. You offer tobacco to these rats and ask them for a tuft of their hair. You braid it into your hair. That'll make you nimble like they are. Give you a chance if you need it."

"I never heard that one before."

"Yeah, well, it ain't strictly ours, eh? That one's from Africa. I learned it from that black nurse works with me midwifing. We trade stuff sometimes. Don't matter. All the same medicine. You just use it, you hear? Spirit rats or flesh and blood rats, they'll give you what you need. They're here to help."

"Yes, Auntie."

I promised to call her tomorrow and made her promise not to tell my mother, not to tell my brothers, for what good it would do. I know how gossip passed around out on the rez. Wouldn't be long before everybody knew what was going on at my house. Which maybe wasn't such a bad thing. Get a few of the old timers burning tobacco for me. Long as my brother Jimmy didn't find out. He'd be over wanting to kick some white man's butt.

I went out and offered my tobacco and found a tuft of rat fur up on the windowsill. I braided it in my hair. I picked the herbs. I drank the tea. I smudged the house. I put the red blanket on the bed.

It was Sunday the next day, and I knew John'd be out drinking with his buddies late that night. It could go either way. Maybe he'd just come home and pass out. Maybe he'd come home mean. I slept with one eye open, tucked up under the protection blanket. I didn't see no rats, but didn't know if that was a good thing or a bad. Rats abandon a sinking ship, or a house where there's a fire coming.

I heard the truck skid through the gravel around 3:00 a.m. He was drunk as a cowboy after a long dry cattle drive. He came in the kitchen, slamming stuff around and stumbling and cursing as he barked his shins and banged his elbows. I heard him pissing in the bathroom, then heard him coming down the hall. He stood in the doorway a few minutes, swaying. I knew he couldn't see my open eyes, dark as the room was, and I sure wasn't going to close them, not knowing what was coming. He took a couple of wide-legged steps toward the bed, trying to keep his balance, and finally toppled like a cut pine across my body. I heaved him over and left him snoring on top of the red blanket. Man, he smelled bad. Whiskey and smoke and beer and, although it broke my heart to admit it, some woman other than me.

I got up and went to the living room and cried myself to sleep, dreaming about rats on river rafts and rats in sewer drains and rats caught in traps.

I woke up the next morning to the sound of John puking. I went to fix him some coffee and orange juice, figuring that'd be about all his stomach could handle. I reached into the cupboard to get his favourite mug, the big one with the bucking bronco on the side of it. Sitting in it, with his little pink paws hooked over the top, was the rat.

"Morning, little buddy." I said. The rat jumped out and stood next to the coffeepot. I opened the fridge to get the orange juice. A rat sat on the stack of cheese slices. He did not budge when I reached in. I wondered if he'd learned how to turn the light on in there when the door was closed.

I heard John behind me and turned. He was still in his boots, his jeans, only his shirt was gone, and I guess he'd puked on it. Even mad at him as I was, there was a twinge down in my belly at the sight of his naked chest, all hard muscle, his flat stomach flat, and the line of pale golden hair running down into the top of his jeans. A rat sat on the top of his head, yanking up his hair with its long pointy teeth.

"Oh, man. My head's killing me." His eyes were blood-shot and yellowish, like two ketchup-covered eggs with runny yolks.

"Serves you right." I wanted him to be hurting. I handed him his coffee. The rat on his head jumped off and disappeared into the living room.

"I ain't in the mood, Nell."

"But I guess you were in the mood last night." I stood with my hands on my hips. I could feel the hurt starting to switch around to righteous anger. I knew I should keep my mouth shut, but I was too mad, too hurt.

"Leave it alone." His voice was ragged and dangerous.

"I don't want to leave it alone. You smelled like a god-damn whorehouse when you came in last night, you bastard. I want to know who you been with!" Out of the corner of my eye, I saw flurries of rat fur. Rats dove under counters, through the window, skittered around door jams and out of the room.

He slammed the cup down on the table, sloshing the coffee over the rim. His hands balled up into fists. He leaned towards me.

"Well, you can bet your fat ass it was somebody under 200 pounds."

Tears sprang to my eyes.

"Look at yourself, you think any man'd want you?" He ran his eyes up and down my body and sneered. "You used to be a good-looking woman, but now you ain't nothing but a sack of lard."

"I am a good wife to you, John McBride. I can't help it if I gained weight."

"What the hell do you mean, you can't help it? I ain't the one stuffing food down your throat! If you'd get off your floppy ass and do some work around this place, maybe you'd lose some of it, maybe I'd want you again!"

"I do all the work around this place! You don't spend long enough here to do no work."

"You saying I'm to blame for how disgusting you got? You blaming me, bitch?"

He took two steps toward me and I backed up until I found myself up against the counter.

"I ain't blaming you, but goddamn, John, it ain't me who's the problem here – it's you!" I couldn't stop myself. "Out whoring around, mean drunk all the time – I ain't gonna take it no more, you understand?"

I didn't see the blow coming.

Even with the rat fur charm braided in my hair, I could not duck the first punch, or the second, or the one after that. Then I lost count. He went for my face, I guess, because it would be the place where the hurt would show the most. Proof that there was some small spot in the world where he could have an effect. My nose. My lips. My cheeks.

I went down, and, a gal my size . . . well, I went down hard and stayed down. I could see his boots in flashes of motion, misted in red.

I think it was all this flesh that saved me from getting worse than I got, and that was bad enough. But I was bundled way down deep inside the womb of myself and even though his hands left bruises, they didn't break no bones. It didn't hurt. I kept thinking it should hurt more, but it just felt like numbness everywhere, great stains of frozen places bursting out from under his icy fists and feet.

"John, John . . ." I just kept repeating in a whisper. My heart speaking to his, willing him to hear me, see me, to stop . . . *you're breaking me,* I thought, *you're breaking me apart.* Then everything went quiet.

I could hear ragged breathing, great gulps of wet sobbing air. I thought it was me, but my moans were underneath that lung-punctured sound. I took my hands away from my face and as I did I heard my Auntie's voice, steel strong and even.

"You step back, John McBride. Step back now."

I looked up at my husband. He stood over me, his face a twisted, crooked thing. Tears poured down his cheeks. His stomach heaved. He looked down at me as though he had no idea of how I'd fallen. He brought his bloody fists up in front of his own eyes and began to howl like a wild dog. He pounded his own face, first with his right hand, then his left, sparing no force.

"Bastard!" he cried, "Bastard!"

"Stop this! Stop this now! You hear me!" Auntie Betty stood in the doorway behind John. She filled the space with her square bulk. Her long grey braid was decorated with *megis* shells. She was dressed for serious ceremony work – ribbons in her spirit colours on her skirt and blouse, medicine pouch at her waist. In her left hand she carried the hawk-wing fan, in her right the sweetgrass basket containing her pipe, tobacco, other things known only to her.

John hit himself square in the face with both fists.

Auntie Betty put her basket down and walked up behind him. She reached up and smacked him on the back of the head.

"Don't be any more of a jackass than you already are. There's been enough hitting for one day, eh?" She glared at him as he spun around. She raised the hawk-wing fan and fluttered a circle in the air around his head. John let out a strangled noise, clamped his hand to his mouth and pushed past her out the door. I heard retching noises.

"Good. Puke up all that bad stuff," said Auntie Betty, coming toward me. "Come on, little one, let's see what kind of shape you're in." She bent down and helped haul me to my feet. I was shaky. There was blood on my dress, dripping down from my nose.

"Looks like I got here just in time. You'll live. Could hear it in the wind this morning. Time to come visit. Had Jimmy drop me off in the truck down the road a ways. Didn't think this'd be the time for him to come calling." She leaned me up against the counter and ran the tap water good and cold. She wet a tea towel and put it in my hand. "Press that up against your face. You need ice." She waddled her wide, bowlegged walk to the fridge.

I started to cry, salty tears burning into my split lip. I heard the tires of our pickup squeal as John skidded out the drive and down the road.

"Don't waste your time crying, girl." She rolled ice in a plastic baggy. "Here, use this. What we need is a cup of tea. He's not coming back for a while. I guarantee. Sit," she ordered, and I did as I was told as she puttered around my kitchen and fixed the tea. She reached into her basket and took out a skin pouch, sprinkled some herbs into the teapot. "This'll help the hurts, inside and out."

I didn't feel much of anything just then, except glad Auntie Betty was there, glad someone else was taking control of things. I felt as limp as a newborn baby and just as naked. We drank the tea. I held the ice to my swelling eye. Auntie Betty held my hand.

Later she reached into her basket.

"I brought this for you," she said, and laid a carton of rat poison on the counter. "You got yourself a vermin problem."

"Poison?" I knew Auntie would never suggest such a thing, it went against the natural respect she had for all-her-relations: spirit rats or full bone and fur. "I don't need that," I said, my chest tight as a drum.

"I think you do. You got these kinda rats, you got to get rid of 'em. White man's rats need white man's measures. This here's white man's poison."

"You can't be serious. You've lost your mind!"

"No, and you better remember to respect your elders! I ain't lost my mind, but you better start using yours. I ain't talking about poisoning nobody, not that some people don't deserve it," she snorted, "but I been giving it some thought. Rat spirit chose to show up here, not no other. No bear or wolf or snake. "

"You're scaring me, Auntie, and I been scared enough for one day."

"Well, let it be the last day anything scares you. You shed that fear skin and maybe you'll shed that fat skin, too. Oh, don't look at me that way, you know it's true. Big woman's a fine thing, but not the way you're going at it. You can't grow another baby in you by trying to stuff it down your mouth. You weren't meant to be as big as you are, you ain't got the bones for it, not like me." She patted her belly and cackled. "But that'll take care of itself once you start taking care of yourself, and for now, that means getting rid of this big old rat."

"He didn't mean it. You saw how sorry he was. It's the pressure. We been going through some hard times."

"What a load of horse shit! Times is always hard. That ain't no excuse for what that man's doing. He needs to learn."

"I can't leave him."

"You can and you will. He might be able to get away with taking out his shit on soft-minded little white women, but no Indian woman's gonna stand for it." She leaned over and took both my hands in hers, looked into my battered-up face.

"You think he's gonna stop unless you make him stop? You think it's not going to just get worse? Don't you watch Oprah?"

I didn't say nothing.

"Nellie. Answer me. You think it's gonna get any better unless he knows he's gone too far, knows exactly what it's cost him? Look me in the eye and tell me that."

She was right. I knew she was right and it caved in my heart to know it.

"I know."

"Well, then."

"But Auntie, I . . ."

"Don't you even think about telling me you love that man! The man you fell in love with is gone. I don't know whether he'll be back or not, but what you got living in this house with you at the moment, sure as hell is not a man to love. This is an evil thing, all twisted over on itself. "I made a motion to protest. "Don't interrupt me. Sometimes you put poison out for rats and like magic they disappear. Seems like they know it just ain't safe no more." She looked at me, her eyes flashing like stars among the wrinkles. "You understand?"

And I did.

She stayed all afternoon and as night fell she smudged the house up good. Then she called Jimmy and had him pick her up. She waited out at the end of the driveway so he wouldn't come in and see me. Jimmy'd be just as likely to go off into town with his rifle and look for John, and nobody wanted that kind of trouble.

John didn't come home that night, and I shouldn't have expected him because Auntie Betty'd told me as much. Still, I lay in bed all night straining to hear the sound of his tires on the gravel. I finally fell asleep around dawn, too tired to mind the aches and pains, and didn't dream about nothing at all.

The next day I fasted. I smudged the house again. Around my neck I put the leather pouch with the lightning stone in it that Auntie'd given me. She'd dug up the round red stone from between the roots of a tree where lightning had struck last spring. It was powerful protection. I wore my ribbon dress. Green ribbons, white ribbons, black and rose. This was my ceremony.

I fixed the food just so. All the things John liked. Fried chicken. Lima beans. Mashed potatoes. Carrot salad with raisins.

I heard the truck in the yard just before 6:00. I took a deep breath. Smoothed my hair. Said a prayer. I heard the screen door shut and then John was in the kitchen. He stood in the doorway, a bunch of red roses in his hand. He was wearing the shirt I'd given his brother Philip last Christmas, so I knew where he'd spent the night. His hair was combed down neat. He looked like a school kid showing up at my door to pick me up for a date.

"Jesus, Nellie, I'm so sorry. I'm gonna spend the rest of my life making it up to you, I swear." He winced when he looked at me. My left eye was swollen and black, my lips were swollen, my cheek had a big bruise on it. I looked a mess. He didn't mention my clothes, although I was in what he called "Squaw gear."

"Come on, baby. You just got to forgive me. It'll never happen again, I mean it, cross my heart. Here, sweetheart." He held out the flowers. I took them but didn't say nothing. I put them in the sink. He came to put his arms around me from behind. I cringed as he squeezed my bruised ribs.

"Don't," I said.

"Okay, okay. I'm sorry." He put his hands up like I was holding a gun on him and backed away. "Christ. I really am sorry, baby. I don't know what got into me. You know how much I love you."

"I fixed some food for you. Fried chicken. Your favourites," I said.

"Oh, honey, you're just the best. I knew you wouldn't stay mad at me." He hugged me and this time I let him. His arms felt so good. For a second I felt safe there. Then I pushed him away.

"Sit down."

John swung his long leg over the back of the chrome chair and sat, a grin on his face. I opened the oven and brought the plate I'd kept warming over to him. Then I went back and leaned up against the kitchen counter, next to the open box of rat poison. He picked up his knife and fork.

"Where's yours?" he said.

"I'm not eating. This here's special food. Just for you, eh?"

"I don't want to eat alone, sugar."

"But I want you to."

He looked puzzled. He looked down at his plate. Looked back over to me and then his eyes flicked to the box of poison. The colour drained out of his face.

"No," he said.

"Why not?" I asked, folding my arms against my chest.

"You eat it," he said.

"Fine," I said. "See, it just don't matter to me anymore." I made a move toward the table, leaned over the plate, brushing my heavy breasts against his shoulder. I took the fork out of his hand and shovelled up a gob of mashed potatoes. I chewed it up and swallowed. He looked at me. I offered him the fork.

"Go ahead," I said.

"No. Eat some of the chicken."

I cut off a piece of chicken and ate it. "Um, um. I sure am a good cook. Yessir. That's one thing you're gonna miss."

He pushed his chair away from the table and stood up.

"What're you talking about?"

"I'm going home, John. I'm leaving you." I felt it then. Knew my heart had just broken.

"You ain't going nowhere." The colour rushed back into his face, his eyes dark and cloudy.

"Yes, I am. And, John McBride, you're going to let me walk out that door and drive back to where you found me. You know why?" I walked back over to the counter and stood near the poison. "Because if you don't, you will never eat another meal in this house without wondering. You will never get another good night's sleep."

"Bitch!" he said, in a rush of air like he'd been punched. He made a move toward me.

I stood my ground, drew myself up and out, became full of myself and my own spirits.

"You will never hit me again and live." I spoke very slowly, softly. "Is this what you want to be doing when you go to meet your maker, John?"

He heard me. I watched my husband's face crumple. He slumped down on the chair and put his head in his hands.

"Don't leave me. I'm begging you. Don't go."

I walked into the bedroom and picked up the bag I'd packed that afternoon. I carried it back into the kitchen. I picked up the keys to the truck from where he'd left them on the hook beside the door.

"You take care now," I said. "I'll have Jimmy drop the truck back later." I closed the door behind me, and started walking, but I could still hear him crying. I stopped by the shed and put down a tobacco tie and some corn and seed for the rats, saying thank you. I didn't see them, but I knew they were around.

Walking to the truck was like wading through hip-deep mud, but I made it. I drove down the road back to the rez and felt like I was dragging my heart all the way, tied to the back of the bumper like an old tin can.

# ACKNOWLEDGEMENTS

I am enormously grateful to everyone at Exile Editions – Barry Callaghan, Michael Callaghan, Priscila Uppal, Chris Doda, and Claire Weissman Wilks – for years of loyalty, support, and encouragement, in an industry where there is precious little of that sort of thing. Thanks, too, to Meaghan Strimas for her careful eye and insightful suggestions.

To Kim Witherspoon, David Forrer and Nathanial Jacks at Inkwell Management – my deepest thanks. Your steadfast belief in me, your work on my behalf, and your wise counsel are as water to the thirsty.

The following stories originally appeared in *Exile: The Literary Quarterly:* "Dirty Money," "An Unrehearsed Desire," "For Marlene, Who Became a Bear," and "Neighbours."

An earlier version of "Last Cup of Tea with Ben" originally appeared in *StoryQuarterly*, and an early version of "The Pretty" appeared in *Matrix*.

"Rat Medicine" and "In the Memory House" were originally published by Mosaic Press in my collection, *Rat Medicine & Other Unlikely Curatives*. I have made certain subtle, but I think important, changes to the text and am delighted to have them included here.

And to R. – faith-keeper, North Star, sanctuary – thank you.

Lauren B. Davis was born in Montreal, and now lives in Princeton, New Jersey, after spending a decade in France with her husband, Ron. Lauren is the author of the best-selling and critically acclaimed novels, *The Radiant City* – a finalist for the Rogers Writers Trust Fiction Prize – and *The Stubborn Season* – chosen for the Robert Adams Lecture Series – as well as a collection of highly praised short stories, *Rat Medicine & Other Unlikely Curatives*. Her short fiction has also been shortlisted for the CBC Literary Awards. Lauren is a mentor with the Humber College School for Writers, Toronto, and Writer-in-Residence at Trinity Church, Princeton. For more information, please visit her website at: *www.laurenbdavis.com*

This book is entirely printed on FSC certified paper.